I Gave My Heart To A Jersey Killa 2

Tina J

Copyright 2019

Warning:

This book is strictly Urban Fiction and the story is **NOT**

REAL!

Characters will not behave the way you want them to; nor will

they react to situations the way you think they should. Some of

them may be drug addicts, kingpins, savages, thugs, rich, poor,

ho's, sluts, haters, bitter ex-girlfriends or boyfriends, people

from the past and the list can go on and on. That is what Urban

Fiction mostly consists of. If this isn't anything you foresee

yourself interested in, then do yourself a favor and don't read it

because it's only going to piss you off. □□

Also, the book will not end the way you want so please be

advised that the outcome will be based solely on my own

thoughts and ideas. I hope you enjoy this book that y'all made

me write. Thanks so much to my readers, supporters, publisher

and fellow authors and authoress for the support. □□

Author Tina J

More books from me:

The Thug I Chose 1, 2 & 3

A Thin Line Between Me and My Thug 1 & 2

I Got Luv For My Shawty 1 & 2

Kharis and Caleb: A Different Kind of Love 1 & 2

Loving You Is A Battle 1 & 2 & 3

Violet and The Connect 1 & 2 & 3

You Complete Me

Love Will Lead You Back

This Thing Called Love

Are We In This Together 1,2 &3

Shawty Down To Ride For a Boss 1, 2 &3

When A Boss Falls in Love 1, 2 & 3

Let Me Be The One 1 & 2

We Got That Forever Love

Aint No Savage Like The One I Got 1&2

A Queen and A Hustla 1, 2 & 3

Thirsty For A Bad Boy 1&2

Hassan and Serena: An Unforgettable Love 1&2

Caught Up Loving A Beast 1, 2 & 3

A Street King And His Shawty 1 & 2

I Fell For The Wrong Bad Boy 1&2

I Wanna Love You 1 & 2

Addicted to Loving a Boss 1, 2, & 3

I Need That Gangsta Love 1&2

Creepin With The Plug 1 & 2

All Eyes On The Crown 1,2&3

When She's Bad, I'm Badder: Jiao and Dreek, A Crazy

Love Story 1,2&3

Still Luvin A Beast 1&2

Her Man, His Savage 1 & 2

Marco & Rakia: Not Your Ordinary, Hood Kinda Love 1,2

& 3

Feenin For A Real One 1, 2 & 3

A Kingpin's Dynasty 1, 2 & 3

What Kinda Love Is This: Captivating A Boss 1, 2 & 3

Frankie & Lexi: Luvin A Young Beast 1, 2 & 3

A Dope Boys Seduction 1, 2 & 3

My Brother's Keeper 1. 2 & 3

C'Yani & Meek: A Dangerous Hood Love 1, 2 & 3

When A Savage Falls for A Good Girl 1, 2 & 3

Eva & Deray 1 & 2

Blame It On His Gangsta Luv 1 & 2

Falling For The Wrong Hustla 1, 2 & 3

I Gave My Heart To A Jersey Killa 1, 2 & 3

Previously…

Ariel

"The new place is ready. You wanna come see it with me?" Armonie wiped her eyes and shook her head yes.

"Awww bookie come here." I hugged her and she broke down crying harder.

"What's wrong?" She moved away and ran in the bathroom to grab tissue.

"Besides me falling in love with someone else's man, not much."

"Huh? Please don't tell me it's my cousin." I had my fingers on the bridge of my nose.

"Ok. I won't. Let's go." She grabbed her things and left me standing there looking crazy. I glanced down at my phone and saw Haven calling me.

"Yea." I closed the door and walked out slowly. I didn't want Armonie hearing us speak.

We haven't gotten the chance to discuss how me and Haven got together. Everyone knew we were messing around now because of her shouting it at the station but no one knew we damn near stayed together.

"You coming over tonight or am I coming to you?" He asked in the phone causing me to smile.

"Let me call you back later."

"Ariel it's either me and you tonight or I can go to the top four on my list."

"Haven, I don't have time to be dealing with your mother because I stabbed you." He busted out laughing.

"Something happened with Armonie. I'm trying to find out."

"What's wrong with her."

"Boy calm down. She's in love with someone else and it ain't Freddy."

"About damn time. I hope the dude thorough." I wanted to tell him my cousin is thorough, and he knows first hand but until Armonie confirmed her and VJ, I wasn't gonna make assumptions.

"I'm sure he is. I'll call you back."

"A'ight." He hung up and I laughed.

We've been sleeping together for the last few months and the feelings have developed for me but I don't want to tell him. He's not tryna be in a relationship and as far as I know, I'm the only chick he's been with. He's waiting on me after work and makes me stay with him when I'm off.

When he leaves the house, he's usually back within an hour or two and we fucking. If there is someone else, she ain't getting what I am and that's attention, his time and the keys to his place.

I felt a little uncomfortable at first accepting the key because his ex used to be here a lot. Then I remembered we've been around one another for years. I did make him get a new bedroom set because I wasn't sleeping in no other woman's bed. He gave me a hard time but then handed me the money and made me get it.

He is definitely spoiled when it comes to sex with me. Both of us are addicted to the other and to be honest, he's the best I've ever had. If you go by his name, you'd assume he was shitty in bed but it's far from the truth.

"How you in love with VJ when y'all barely around one another?" I asked and started my car. I had to pry.

"It's a long story and right now I just wanna lay down. Can you pull over?" I did and she vomited on the ground.

"What the hell did you eat?"

"I think it's because I'm so upset. You know how I get." I nodded because growing up if Monie stressed herself out too much, she'd throw up. The doctor said she has acid reflux when she worked herself up or some shit.

"VJ is a good guy Monie but he's taken and so are you."

"Not anymore. I broke up with Freddy but you're right. He's taken and I never should've gotten caught up." I handed her a napkin and pulled off.

"Caught up?" I wanted to ask if they had sex because I know like she did, Freddy would flip if he knew someone else took what he's been waiting years for.

"Yea. We'll talk later. I'm getting a headache."

"Ok." I left it alone and drove to the new house I got us. My dad had some being built and let me pick one. He said I needed a home and not a condo.

"Where are we?"

"At our new house." She stared at me.

"House? Ariel you know we were only staying in the condo until we got married. We made a pact to purchase a house when we had a family." She's right. Neither of us wanted to live in a house with no one to share it with. She has money and could purchase her own, but I enjoy having her as my roommate.

"Let me find out you don't like living with me." We started laughing.

"Anyway, what's up with you and Haven and don't tell me my eyes were deceiving me." She asked getting out the car and walking up to the door with me.

"We having fun."

"Fun my ass. You've been staying out a lot and one night, I swore I heard you moaning out his name in the guest room." I covered my mouth.

11

"I didn't say anything because I was half sleep but now I see it wasn't a dream." She folded her arms.

"Y'all been fucking for a minute."

"Fine! After him and VJ fought, he came by days later and we slept together. He stopped by again and we've been sharing a bed ever since." I unlocked the door.

"Ok now." She glanced around the house from the doorway.

"Am I gonna have some little Reaper cousins soon." She rubbed my stomach.

"Hell to the no. We use condoms and both of us check when we done to make sure it didn't bust."

"Are y'all a couple?" She asked and stepped in with me. I closed the door and we walked around the place.

"No." She stopped and turned around.

"Are you expecting anything from him as far as being a couple?"

"To be honest, I wouldn't mind him being my man but he told me straight up he's not ready to be in a committed relationship."

"Ariel." She had a sad look on her face.

"I know I deserve better."

"You do sis. I love my cousin but he's gonna mess up and you seem like you're feeling him a lot. I don't want you to get hurt like me."

"Like you?" She snickered like a school girl.

"Haven may not be committed to anyone, but he loves sleeping with different women. We both know that. Ariel, you're about to graduate and there's more good men out there who will treat you better."

"Damn Armonie. You sound like me talking to you." We shared a laugh.

"He threatened me already." She stopped.

"I can't be with anyone else and I don't wanna place anyone in danger because he doesn't care."

"So you're in the same situation as me; only he doesn't beat on you and gonna kill you if another man fucks you. Let me find out you threw it on my cousin."

"What can I say?" We gave each other a high five and finished going through the house. I dropped her off at the hotel because she wanted to make sure the room was cleaned. I never did ask about the stuff with my cousin. Oh well, I'll ask tomorrow.

****

"Hey." Haven answered on the first ring. I closed the computer down and focused my attention on the conversation I was about to have.

"Baby, I passed my exam. One more and I'll be a RN." I all but shouted on the phone.

I was now walking outta work and I knew he was at the club because there's a party. He asked me if I was coming but getting off at 11 and going home to get dressed would be too much. I decided to sit this one out and wait for him at his house like always.

"That's good. Real good." He said but something about the way he said it made my antennas go up.

"Where are you? I wanna celebrate and you know how." I hit the alarm on my car and sat down.

"Got dammit." I heard shuffling in the background.

"What's wrong?" It sounded as if he fell.

14

"My phone dropped. I'll hit you up later." I didn't respond, hung the phone up and pulled off. Haven thinks I'm stupid but let's see if my intuition is correct.

I drove straight to my old condo, took a fast shower, threw on some dressy shit and hauled ass to the club. Armonie and I hired movers to come this weekend and since she's staying at her parents, I didn't want to stay here alone, which is why I've been staying with Haven.

I parked in the back of the club and prayed the side door was open. When I realized it wasn't, I had to save face and go through the front. There was no line because it was after 12 in the morning which meant everyone who was coming is probably already there.

The guy at the front door must've been new because I've never seen him, and he didn't ask if I was looking for Haven like the rest of the security did.

The place was packed and I had to maneuver in and out of people to get by. I stopped when I noticed security at the stairs leading up to Haven's office. I had one of two choices. Take my chances and see if they let me up or yell out somebody has a gun and hope they move. I went with the latter and shit became chaotic. Security stayed put but moved up closer to see what was going on, giving me easy access to go up the stairway.

I prepared myself for what I'm about to see because after hanging up on Haven, I tried calling back a few more times and he didn't answer. Again, I'm no fool so watching this naked woman giving him head shouldn't surprise me. I don't even wanna think about them having sex, which may have already taken place but fuck it.

"Shit girl. Suck all of it out." He moaned with his head back and eyes closed.

"This is why you couldn't answer the phone for me?"

"Oh shit." Haven jumped up and the girl wiped her mouth.

"Haven, I didn't know you had a girl."

"He doesn't. I'm not sure why he stopped you." He sat there staring at me.

"Can you give us a minute?" Haven said continuing to keep his eyes on me.

"Sure. Don't be long because I'm tryna ride that ride again tonight." She grabbed her clothes and stepped out. I'm not even mad at her.

"Drained?" I questioned as he sat there with his dick still out. I closed the door and shook my head.

"You know my father said to leave you alone because you weren't ready. Armonie said you were gonna hurt me but noooo. I had to be hardheaded and continue messing with you." I picked up the Tito's bottle and poured me a drink.

"Do you mind putting your dick away? I don't wanna see her slob all over it." He fixed himself and stood.

"I should've left you alone when I caught feelings because like you said, love don't live here anymore right." I used my index finger to poke where his heart is.

"You told me I was number one in your top five and I laughed it off. There's no way you had a top anything because we were always together." I poured another shot and tossed it back.

"Do you know when I got the results for my exam, you were the first person I called. My parents don't even know yet." I took another shot.

"You seemed happy but then I don't know if you telling me that's good, was meant for me or the BITCH YOU WERE IN HERE FUCKING!"

CRASH! I tossed the bottle against the door.

"I'm a damn good woman Haven and whether you say it or not, I deserve better." The tears started racing down my face.

"Better than a man who can't claim me. A man who has a got damn top five, ten or whatever. A man who cares about no one but himself. And a man who can't even look me in my face knowing he fucked up." He sat in his chair continuing to do other shit and not speak.

"I've never been a woman to act out over a man. I hate who you made me into." I grabbed my purse and stormed towards the door.

"Remember what I said about you being with someone else." Is what he managed to say. I turned and he was now staring at me.

"I don't give a fuck about you being the reaper Haven. I'm going to find me a good man. Someone to treat me better and build with. If you wanna kill me in the process, go ahead. Walking in on the man I fell in love with getting his dick sucked has already killed me inside. Goodbye." I slammed the door, walked to the stairs and went tumbling down.

"Shit. You ok?" One of the security guys helped me up.

"I'm fine. Can you open the side door for me?" He did and it felt like my arm was about to fall off. It had to be broken. He asked if I wanted him to walk me to my car and I declined. Haven would probably murder him for being nice.

I walked alone and unlocked the door. When I checked my arm is was black and blue and already swelling up. I drove down the street and called Armonie. She was half sleep but woke up when I mentioned needing the hospital. I told her where I was and twenty minutes later, she drove me to the ER.

"You want me to stay with you?" She asked when the nurse came in to take me to X-ray.

"No sis. I'm ok. I'll call you when I get home." She hugged me and I told her I'd take an Uber and pick my car up tomorrow. After three hours in the ER, I ended up with a broken arm and dislocate finger.

"What happened to you?" I sucked my teeth at Eddie who was standing there.

"Stop the attitude Ariel. I messed up by promoting those lies but I do care about you." I blew my breath and took a seat on the bench while I waited for the Uber.

"Let me take you home." I rolled my eyes.

"I'm serious. It's the least I can do." He smiled and I laughed. I canceled the Uber and waited for him to pull the car around. He helped me in and off to my condo I went. Haven had the nerve to call me back to back. I shut my phone off. *Fuck him.*

Haven

"Clean this shit up." I told the janitor who was here cleaning up after the club closed. Ariel threw the bottle against the door and glass was everywhere. Usually he came during the day, but he requested tomorrow off, which is really today. He had to take his wife to the hospital for tests.

"Ok sir. I don't want no problems." He put his hands up.

"My bad yo. I'm not mad at you." I said and handed him $100. He tried to give it back three times until I yelled.

"Girl problems." He laughed.

"Something like that." I picked up my drink and took a sip as I stared down on the empty dance floor.

After Ariel left outta here crying, I stayed in my office for the remainder of the night. Marlena tried to come back to fuck again but I told security not to let her up. My head was messed up after seeing Ariel hurting. All the years Juicy and I were together she's never caught me with another woman. Why do the words I hate you hurt when someone says it?

I definitely had strong feelings for Ariel, but I kept pushing them away. I didn't wanna fall hard and she does me the same as me ex. Brayden told me to leave her alone if I was gonna cheat but I couldn't after getting the first taste. It's like we were addicted to one another. Plus, I didn't want anyone else to have her. Of course it's selfish but I never thought I'd get caught. To be honest, we were together so much lately I didn't have time to be with another woman.

Marlena's a stripper and I've fucked her numerous times. The sex is decent and she's been begging for me to dick her down but I never did. Tonight, the drinks were in my system and I couldn't pass up her fat ass. I'll never blame the alcohol because I'm fully aware of where I stick my dick but it doesn't help when you're being tempted.

"You good?" I asked the janitor. When he said yes, I rushed out to go home to shower and change. I needed to speak with Ariel. She was beyond hurt and the least I could do is explain. I admit she had me at a loss for words but I'm good now.

"Boss, how's Ariel?" One of my security dudes asked. I placed my gun on his temple and his hands went up.

"Tha fuck you mean is she ok? You let her upstairs to catch me with Marlena."

"Oh boss, I didn't know that happened. I was asking because she fell down the steps and one of the other guys came to get me." He said with a concerned look.

"What?" I pulled my gun back.

"They said she rolled down the stairs. I tried to walk her to the car and offered to call someone but she refused."

"Was it bad?"

"Her arm swelled up pretty quick and she cried walking to her car."

"FUCK!" I put the gun in my waist.

"Thanks and my bad for pulling the gun out. I'm going through some shit."

"It's all good. I'll make sure to let your sister know when I get home." I laughed because he's my sister's fiancé. They've been together forever, and he's actually cool as hell. I should've known he wouldn't let me get caught but Ariel had my head fucked up.

"Got damn snitch."

"I'll be that. Also, I accept the invitation to take paid days off." He laughed, hit me up with the peace sign and left.

I picked my phone up and called Ariel back to back. She had the audacity to shut her phone off.

I jumped in my car and raced to the hospital. By the time I got there the nurse said she left twenty minutes ago. I didn't waste time going home and decided to stop by her house. On the way out, I noticed Armonie's car but why is she here? If Ariel is gone, I don't know why she hasn't left. I called her phone and she let it go to voicemail each time. I hit Colby Jr up and had him try to reach her.

I parked in front of Ariel's condo and there was a car behind hers. I never seen it and since Armonie's at the hospital, I know she doesn't have company. I stepped out, walked to the door and used my key to get in. I know they're moving but I still had mine.

There was no one in the living room and I could hear noises coming from upstairs. I took the steps two at a time and went straight to her room. It was like de ja vu all over. Clothes were spread out on the floor and the shower was going.

"I told her not to fuck with no one else and here she is showering with the nigga." I spoke to myself as I followed the clothes in the bathroom.

"Shit." I heard her say and my anger went from 0-1000 real quick. I took my gun out, cocked it back, opened the shower curtain and placed the gun on her head.

"You thought I was playing?"

"HAVEN!" Her eyes got big as hell.

"Nah, it's the fucking Reaper."

VJ

"I know he's fucking the bitch from Jersey and if he's not with the dirty one, it's his cousins' friend." Mecca said to her shiesty ass friend Lily. Yup, the same one who tried to fuck.

"But why you mad when you almost fucked Raheem?"

"Sssssh. Bitch be quiet."

"What's the difference if he is fucking someone?" Lily asked and I waited for the answer.

"The difference is I won't ever sleep with another man. I messed up even allowing Raheem to kiss me but when it comes to touching; absolutely not."

"Kissing is touching."

"Are you on my side?" Mecca asked.

"Oh course. I just don't understand if you feel like he stepping out, then do the same." I stood in the doorway of Mecca's bedroom listening to her talk to her friend.

I returned from Jersey a few days ago and today is the first day I stopped by to see Mecca. Between work and tryna figure out if I wanna move to Jersey, she wasn't on my to do list.

Then, I get here and she wanted to have sex. As soon as I said no, she caught an attitude. I ignored it and fell asleep in the room. I woke up to her and Lily's conversation. It didn't matter to me one way or the other at this point if she were with another man because I'm done.

After spending all that time with Armonie, it only verified me being over Mecca and its not because I took her virginity. Monie was smart, held intelligent conversations and had no problem putting me in my place if I made her mad. The thought of another man touching her is something I never wanna envision which is why I spent my days in Jersey with her. I hadn't broken up with Mecca yet, so I understood why she was upset.

I left her the note because I knew she wouldn't speak to me after her dumb ass ex accused me of sleeping with his sister.

The day he's speaking of was a week before he showed up at the hotel. Mycah and I stopped by some chicken place

27

and Latifa was there. She caught an attitude when I told her to beat it. What do you think she did? Yup, went and flirted with Mycah. He's a straight dog and when she offered the pussy, he took it.

We went to her house, they fucked, and I passed out on the couch from drinking with Freddy's pops. Its crazy how Freddy's dad was cool and he was a fuck nigga.

Long story short, I got up the next day and walked out to start the car. Mycah had already came down and told me she was about to give him some head real quick and he'll be right down.

Freddy was coming in from somewhere and smiled when he saw me. I knew for a fact he wasn't with Monie because I spoke to her the night before and she was staying at her parents. She even called me on facetime as he walked in, still at her parent's place. I wish she would've let me explain but she was too upset. I wasn't sure if she told Ariel yet, so I didn't call and ask her to speak to Monie. I did have Ariel check on her though because she ran out and I couldn't find her.

Its all good though because I'm leaving in a few days to go back to check on her.

Vanity and I had a long conversation and she's moving in a couple weeks. I'm gonna wait an extra month or so and then see where my head is.

"What you doing here Lily?" Mecca jumped and turned around while Lily stuck her finger in her mouth like she was sucking a dick behind her back.

"Came by to check on my girl. I'm out." She grabbed her expensive ass purse and left. I shook my head. I thought she would've been kicked out by now but she came up with the rent for the next couple of months.

"Hey baby. You feel better?" I looked at her.

"There's nothing wrong with me." She ran her hands up my chest from behind.

"You don't usually turn down sex, so I thought something was wrong." I turned to her and stared.

"We're finished Mecca." She backed away.

"What?"

"You heard me. This relationship is over."

"Why now? Is it because you found someone in Jersey?" I popped the top off the water bottle and took a sip.

"Why you say that?"

"Because we were on good terms before going there. Now you're ready to break up. Its obviously someone else."

"Actually, I'm not in love with you and never have been."

"Excuse me." She was definitely offended.

"You heard me. I care and have love for you but that dangerous type of love people have for their significant other isn't there for me." Her mouth fell open. I went in the room to get my stuff.

"I thought it would come eventually but the longer we were together, the further away I felt. All the arguing and fighting over stupid shit took a toll on me too. Then, to hear about this Raheem dude is a blow to my face; especially when we hang around the same crowd."

"No, its because of those bitches in Jersey." I shook my head laughing.

"This is what I mean. I'm tryna talk and tell you why its not working and you assume its someone else." I folded my arms.

"And even if it were someone else, you let her slide right in because all you concerned yourself with is tryna keep me on a leash, when you should've been loving me the right way."

"I... I... don't know what to say." She stood there lost.

"Ain't nothing to say." I glanced around her place.

"I don't have anything here that I can see. If you find something, you can toss it." I opened the front door and bounced. I sat in my car and picked the phone up to facetime Monie. It's been a few days so she should've calmed down by now.

"You better be dying if you're calling me." She spoke with an attitude.

"Whatever. Where are you? Its dark as hell out there and its late." It was after midnight and the time zone is the same.

"None of your business."

31

"Armonie don't play with me." She sucked her teeth and told me at the hospital with Ariel. My cousin fell and she brought her in. Ariel told her she could leave and she did but went back because she felt bad.

"Ok but why you outside?"

"Duh. I was about to get out until this taken man called my phone." She turned her lip up after getting smart. I laughed at her being petty.

"Well this taken man is on the market again." I started my car and placed the phone in the cup holder. She was still on facetime and I'm about to tell her I'll be there soon. We had some making up to do.

"Oh yea? How is that?" I noticed her constantly turning her head.

"I told her I wasn't in love with her. Who are you looking for?" I asked. She was making me nervous and I wasn't even there.

"No one but I feel my car moving; like someone's pushing it."

"WHAT?" My heart started beating fast as hell.

32

"VJ, I think someone is out here."

"Start your car and pull off." She went to do it and outta nowhere, her car door swung open and her body was yanked out. The phone must've fallen because I couldn't see anything, but I could hear.

"Ahhhhh. Please stop. VJJJJJJ! Help me. Please stop." I heard and was about to dial 911 on the other line. I couldn't hang up and something else happened.

BOOM! BOOM! Someone knocked on my window. I looked up and it was Mecca. I put my finger up and dialed 911. I had them on the phone and felt like shit because I didn't know the name of the hospital to send the cops. Monie's phone hung up when I clicked over and it infuriated me more because I had no idea what was going on. I called back over and over but it rang and went to voicemail. I sent Brayden a text asking him to go to the hospital.

BOOM! BOOM! I rolled the window down to a crying Mecca.

"What's up?"

"I love you VJ and I'm not about to let another woman have you."

"Go head Mecca. I got other important things to think about." I turned my head when a notification popped up and felt something sharp digging in the top of my shoulder and then my neck. I turned around and this bitch had a fucking pair of scissors in her hand. I grabbed my neck and blood started pouring out.

"Are you crazy?"

"Crazy over you." The bitch jammed the shit so hard in my collarbone, I thought I was gonna die. I opened my car door and started chasing her with the scissors still in me. The bitch was screaming like a maniac.

"Fuck!" I said to myself as dizziness washed over me. I dropped to my knees and hit the pavement head first.

Mecca

"Shit. Shit. Shit." I yelled out when I ran inside my house.

After VJ announced he was leaving me, I don't think it registered. I mean, I heard him but wasn't sure if he meant it. Then, he left without giving me a hug or even really explaining why he never fell in love. How does a man stay with you for an extended amount of time and not fall in love? What am I missing?

I grabbed the sharpest pair of scissors I had and ran out the house. I assumed he left; yet, there he sat, in his car on FaceTime with the bitch from Jersey just like I suspected. VJ was so engrossed in the conversation he had no idea, I stood there. I'm not sure which hurt more; him leaving me or him running out the house to call her. Whatever the case, when he rolled down the window, I stabbed him repeatedly. It was only a few times in actuality, but it felt like a lot.

I thought he would kill me after jumping out the car. However; the amount of blood pouring out must've slowed him down because he dropped to his knees and then hit the ground. His head bounced off the pavement and as bad as I wanted to check on him, I hauled ass in my house.

I ran in my closet, grabbed a few duffle bags and some garbage bags from the kitchen to pack my things. I threw any and everything in there I could.

By the time I left the house, cops, ambulances and mad people were out there. Silently, I prayed VJ died because if not, I'm gonna need to hide or go on the run. He's not the type to let me use insanity and heat of the moment as the reason I did it. He's definitely going to kill me and if he doesn't, his cousin Brayden will.

VJ isn't in the street life but his cousin and the people he hung with are. If they find out I did this, there's no doubt I'm a dead woman walking.

I can't forget his stuck-up ass sister. The bitch thinks she's better than me, but her hands are serious. I've seen her rock bitches to sleep. The guy she's with have these men out here scared to death to speak to her and he's not even from here. The amount of power and money rolling within those families are ridiculous.

"Ma'am did you see anything?" A cop asked as I put things in my car.

"No sir. What happened?" I pretended not to know.

"A man was stabbed."

"Oh my God. Is he ok?" I put my hand on my chest to play it off.

"It's pretty bad. Not sure if he's going to make it. Are you sure you didn't see anything?" He asked again.

"No. I wish I did. That's horrible. If you'll excuse me." He tipped his hat and allowed me to pass and return inside my place. I picked my phone up, put it against my ear as I grabbed the last of my bags and locked the door.

"What up bitch? I'm about to go on stage." Lily spoke in the phone. I walked back to my car and sat there watching the cops interaction.

"Oh my God. Something happened to VJ outside my house." I used a fake cry and everything.

"What? Are you ok?"

"Yea somebody stabbed him. What if they're gonna come after me?" I should get an award for the way I carried on.

"Shit. Go stay with my cousin and I'll come see you when I'm done."

"Lily we stopped speaking and..." She cut me off.

"I'm about to call him. Just go there."

"Ok. I'm scared Lily."

"You're gonna be fine. Hurry up." I had a huge smile on my face.

"Ok." I played the shit outta my role. I hung up and sat in my car. I watched the cops go around asking more questions and shook my head. After seeing the ambulance pull off, I left too. There's nothing to stay here for.

****

"You a'ight?" Some guy asked outside of the bodega. I stopped here to grab some chips, a soda and condoms. Of course her cousin is gonna want to fuck if I'm staying there. Especially; after the way we ended things and I'm not getting pregnant. What if VJ survives and finds me? I will not leave a child alone in this world.

38

"I'm ok. Thank you." He held the door open and I stepped out. When I got to my car, I realized my phone had a few missed calls and a text message. I opened the text and it read:

Call me Mecca. This is Brayden. I need to know if my cousin is ok. I dialed the number and he answered right away.

"Mecca is my cousin ok?" How did he get my number? He never calls.

"I don't know Brayden. He said he was going to the store and would be back. After a while when he didn't return, I got worried. Some cop knocked on my door and told me there was a stabbing. I go down there and it's VJ."

"WHAT? MY COUSIN GOT STABBED!" He shouted in the phone scaring me.

"Yea. I'm pulling up to the hospital now." I lied my ass off.

"We'll be there shortly." He said in a calm voice. Maybe I am playing this role perfect.

"We?" I questioned. That means all their relatives are coming. I have to get the fuck outta here before he tells VJ's parents because I damn sure ain't calling them.

"Me and my family." I swallowed hard. Shit is gonna get hectic.

"Ok. I'll see you when y'all get here." I went to hang up and heard him speak.

"Oh and Mecca."

"Yea."

"I know about my cousin leaving you and if he tells me you did this, I'm killing you and everyone in your family." My mouth dropped as I stared at the screen saver on the phone.

I sped out the parking lot and drove straight to Lily's cousin house that was an hour away. I should probably leave the state, but I had no money. *FUCK!*

I got out the car, grabbed two bags and walked up the porch.

"You good?" He opened the door before I got to it.

"Yea Raheem and thanks for letting me stay."

"You're mine now." He locked the door behind me. I turned around and stared at how sexy he was.

Please let this be the right decision. I said to myself.

"I guess so." I asked him to grab the rest of my things out the car and if I could use his shower. He told me yes and once the water hit me, so did the stabbing. I let the tears roll down my face thinking about VJ and I never being together and the fact he may die. I should've waited until I calmed down and now look. My life is on the line and there's nothing anyone can do to save me.

"You ok?" Raheem stepped in the shower. I glanced in between his legs and he had a decent size but nothing like VJ. He was hung like a horse, which is why it hurt during sex.

"I'm good." He had me look at him.

"I don't know what happened, but I got you." I nodded and he placed his lips on mine. What we're about to do will relax me for sure. I'll think of my next move tomorrow.

Haven

"Get that fucking gun off my head." She smacked my hand away with her good one. She had plastic covering her other arm. I checked the shower, then the bathroom, along with the rest of the house.

"Who the fuck car outside and why you in here moaning?" She rolled her eyes and continued washing up without saying a word.

"Don't play with me Ariel."

"Ain't nobody in here moaning. I hit my arm against the wall and as you can see, its broke." She raised it for me to see.

"Who car is outside then?" She rolled her eyes.

"Get the fuck out Haven, Reaper or whoever you are." The shower cut off and I handed her a towel. After she dried off the best she could with the plastic bag wrapped around her arm, I tightened it up.

"Why are you here and who I have in my house where I pay bills, is none of your concern."

"Whose fucking car is out there?" She smirked.

"My ex, why? Did you not see him while you were creeping in?" She thought shit was funny.

"I don't have to creep and if he were here, you'd be cleaning up a dead body."

"Oh no Haven. You don't get to kill nobody I decide to sleep with when you're doing it." She started punching me with her good hand.

"Stop Ariel." I grabbed her wrist and she snatched away. I knew she was hurt and I wanted to apologize but the words wouldn't come out.

"Fuck you Haven." She went to her dresser to pull clothes out.

"Why you mad tho? You knew about the top five? I told you in the beginning..."

"Screw your top five bullshit. You fucking me every night, and got the nerve to slide in someone else. I'm not even gonna suggest my pussy must not be good because we know it is." I waved my hand at her.

"You and I have the same sexual appetite Haven; why couldn't you wait until I got off?" She cried wiping her tears as she slid her leg inside the pajama pants.

"I don't even know Ariel. I was drinking and the temptation took over." She sucked her teeth.

"I knew it wasn't you I was fucking and I shouldn't have done it but it's over." I said with finality.

"Exactly. Just like whatever this is we had." I wasn't tryna hear anything she had to say.

"Yea right." I sparked the blunt and lit it.

"You heard me Haven. It's over, finished, done. Go be with that bitch and the others. You can move her to the top spot because I'm done. I deserve better and I'm not sticking around until you figure out the same thing." She picked up some pills and wash them down with water.

"Can you go? These pain pills are gonna kick in shortly and I don't want you anywhere near me." She stood there tapping her foot. I put the blunt down in the ashtray and stood.

"Where's the person whose car is outside?"

"Not that it's your business but my ex brought me home from the hospital." I bit the inside of my jaw to keep from lashing out.

"His girlfriend picked him up, so he left his car. Now go." She pointed to the door.

"I'll be back." I took my sneakers off, then my clothes and hopped in the shower. I never had time to run home because I wanted to check on her. I have things here to put on and if I didn't, I'd sleep naked.

"Go home Haven." She shouted in the bathroom. I ignored her and washed up. I heard everything Ariel said and she deserved better. However; if I'm not giving her better, no other nigga will either.

I stepped out, dried off and walked in the room to see her going through my phone. I shook my head laughing. She wasn't gonna find anything because I hadn't been with anyone else before tonight. Her eyes connected with mine and then hers went back to the phone.

"You done bitching?" I put on a pair of boxers and basketball shorts, picked my blunt up and finished smoking.

"When are you leaving?" She threw the phone at me and laid down. Her eyes were getting heavy and her words were slurring.

"Take yo ass to sleep."

"Fuckkkkk you." She slurred again and fell out. I covered her body and laid next to her. It's always felt right being next to her. I'm not sure why I even took it there with Marlena, but it won't happen again.

****

"Yo! What's up?" I spoke groggily in the phone. I had just dosed off after watching ESPN.

"Get down to the hospital." I sat up listening to Colby sound like he was crying.

"What's wrong? You crying?"

"Somebody tried to kill Armonie. Cuz it don't look good." I almost fell tryna get out the bed.

"I'm on my way."

"A'ight. Tell Ariel." I glanced over at her.

"She's high off pain pills. I'll come back for her." I told him and pulled the covers up on her.

"Pain pills?" He questioned.

"I'll tell you later. I'm on my way." I disconnected the call, hurried to throw some clothes on, kissed Ariel's cheek and hauled ass outta there. I noticed the other car was missing. Dude must've known not to knock on Ariel's door. He's lucky too because I would've murked him.

I sped to the hospital and when I got there all of my family were here. Some were outside and others had to be in the waiting room. Colby Jr. and Jax headed to my car and told me to stay in. They needed to smoke. I unlocked the doors and turned for one of them to speak.

"When you mentioned seeing her car, I called a few times but she didn't answer. I figured she was sleep until I called my mom and asked if she were in the room, since she's been staying there." I nodded.

"Brayden ended up calling me and asked if I knew where she was too, which made me hop out the bed. He said his cousin texted him from Virginia and..." Colby got choked up.

"What?"

"That someone followed her and she needed help. I get here and search the parking lot for her…" I passed the blunt to Jax and Colby closed his eyes.

"She was on the ground bleeding from her body." I let a tear fall down.

"I should've checked on her when I saw the car." I said regretting leaving without checking first.

"Don't blame yourself." Jax said and I let my head fall on the window. How can I not blame myself?

"What are they saying?" I asked.

"The cops searched the video footage and it was dark. You saw someone lurking around the parking lot but they had a half mask on and a hat. You can't tell if it's a girl or guy." Jax said from the backseat.

"Girl?" I asked.

"You know Armonie whooped a lotta bitch's ass." Colby said and he's right. Armonie had a temper on her and would fight at the drop of a dime.

"Lets go before the doctors come out." We stepped out the car and headed back in.

"Let me hit Brayden up." I pulled my phone out.

"When's the last time you checked your phone?" Jax questioned me.

"I haven't really. Some shit kicked off with Ariel and I had to make some moves."

"Got caught cheating already?" Colby said and they both laughed.

"We weren't a couple."

"Shitttttt." They said at the same time.

"All you did was work and hide out with her. Y'all were a couple even though you tryna deny it." Jax said laughing. They knew how Ariel and I were because they've been to the house when she's been there.

"What the fuck ever." I waved them off.

"Anyway, Brayden drove to Virginia with his family because someone stabbed his cousin." I stopped walking.

"Not the kung fu nigga."

"Yup him." Colby laughed.

"He got beef down there." I asked.

"Brayden thinks his girl did it." Jax chimed in.

49

"What am I missing?"

"Obviously a whole lot." Jax said and we stepped in the hospital. My aunt Journey was sitting on uncle Colby's lap crying. My mom, dad and everyone else were waiting around to hear something; anything.

"The family of Armonie Banks." The doctor surveyed the waiting room and his eyes got big as hell when all of us stood.

"I'm her mom, he's her dad and this is all of her family. How is she?" He pointed to a chair and asked her to sit.

"It's was touch and go for a minute. There were a few stab wounds on her body but luckily for her, the person didn't harm the baby."

"BABY!" All of us shouted at the same time.

"Yes, she's about twelve weeks." The entire room remained quiet.

"Told you she was fucking." My father said and my mom smacked him on the arm.

"I have her on antibiotics to make sure there's no infection from the stab wounds. Also, whoever did this must've punched her quite a bit because she has busted vessels in her eye and her nose is bruised really bad. Not broken but she still has to be careful with it."

"Can we see her?" My aunt Journey asked.

"She's in ICU so only two at a time can go in." No one even questioned who would go first as my uncle Colby and Journey walked behind him.

"Haven, I don't care who this person's family is. I want them all dead when you find out who it is and Colby Jr., you and Jax are to find that Freddy dude. How the hell he get her pregnant and let her keep it a secret?" My father said. We all nodded and took a seat. Everyone wanted to see Armonie with their own eyes to make sure she's ok.

"What up Brayden?" I answered my phone and stepped out the door.

"Everything good down there?"

"Armonie's ok; fucked up pretty bad but good." I told him.

"How's your cousin?" I asked not really caring but he asked about mine.

"We don't know yet. Whoever did this, stabbed him so deep they hit nerves. His arm may be fucked up permanently."

"Damn. Now I have to take it easy on him when we fight." He started laughing. I have no doubt me and dude will get into it again.

"You think they're connected?" He asked.

"I don't even know bro. Shit is crazy though."

"Yea. How's my sister?" He asked about Ariel.

"She fell and broke her arm. I was gonna bring her but she high as fuck off the pain pills. She's gonna be out for a while. I'm bringing her up in the morning."

"How did she fall?" I explained a little of what went down. Well, I told him she came to see me and fell down the steps. I left Marlena out because I didn't want them worrying about her when they got other issues.

"Please watch her Haven. I know shit is hectic with your cousin and we're going through the same, but we don't know what's going on. Neither of our families can take anymore right now." He loved his sister, so I'm not even offended he asked.

"I got her. Let your parents know she good and I'll have her call you in the morning."

"A'ight. Talk to you later." We hung up and I walked back in the hospital and sat next to Colby and Jax. They asked me what happened with his cousin.

"Somebody stabbed him deep and he may lose movement in his arm." I told them.

"Damn." Colby said shaking his head.

"I know right."

"Can y'all believe Armonie pregnant?" Jax said.

"Hell no. I ain't even know she was fucking. She wasn't beat for Freddy. What if it's not his?" We looked at Colby.

"I'm just saying."

"Is she ok?" The manager from her hotel ran in full of tears.

"How did you find out?" Jax asked. She pointed outside to the local news station. They were reporting live.

"Did you call her boyfriend? He's gonna be devastated."

"Fuck Freddy. He don't need to know about..." Colby tried to say but she cut him off.

"Freddy?" She questioned confusing all of us.

"No this guy beat Freddy up the other day at the hotel. I mean damn near killed him." All of us looked at her.

"Who was he?" Colby Jr. stood up and backed her against the wall.

"I don't know. He's not from here though."

"How you know it's her man then?" Now I started questioning her.

"He's been to the hotel a lot. They went to the pool together, ate at the restaurant and a few times they went to the theatre. You sure y'all don't know about him? He's been here for a couple months." She asked and looked at the three of us. My father walked over and so did my aunt Venus.

"Was he tall, handsome with a goatee? He spoke with an accent too." My aunt Venus asked.

"Yes. Very southern like."

"Hmph. She went ahead and took him from his bitch." Venus said and smirked.

"Huh?" Colby Jr asked this time.

"Ariel's cousin came in the shop to get his girl a while back. His bitch was popping shit so I told Monie to take him from her. Who knew she do it and they'd take it there?" She smirked.

"Ariel's cousin?" It was my turn to ask questioned because it's no way in hell she's speaking of VJ.

"Yea. The one who fought those guys at the restaurant when you were acting a fool." My aunt Venus never had a problem talking shit to any of us. Ariel must've told her what happened because they're tight.

"VJ?" All three of us shouted.

"Yea that's him. He's in love with Armonie. Make sure you call him because he's gonna want to be here." The chick from the hotel said.

"You gotta be fucking kidding me." I stepped out to call Brayden.

"Hey. Did Armonie wake up?" He asked soon as he picked up.

"Bro. I'm gonna ask this question and I need you to keep it a hundred." There was silence.

"It's true." I hadn't even asked yet.

"How you know what I was about to ask?"

"He mentioned it the day he left. It's why he broke up with Mecca and planned on moving here. He fucked around and fell in love with Armonie, which is why I'm gonna tell him she's ok until he's better."

"Did you know she's pregnant too?"

"What?"

"Yea. Twelve weeks. We just found out." I stared at the dark sky.

"Oh shit. Nah, I didn't know, and I doubt he knows because he would've told me." I didn't say a word.

"Is it your cousins?" I asked because none of us wanted Freddy in her life. If she were pregnant by him, we'd be stuck with him around forever.

"If she's pregnant like you say, then yes. He was her first and those two were together a lot. Shit. I was shocked when he told me Ariel doesn't even know yet."

56

"Damn she really kept him a secret." I shook my head.

"Yea. Let me hit you back. The doctor just came out." He said.

"A'ight. I got your sister."

"Thanks." We hung up and I went in to wait to see Armonie. What a day?

Armonie

"Who would do this to her?" I heard my mom crying and opened my eyes. She was on my father's lap with her head on his shoulders. My body was in extreme pain and all I wanted to do is go back to sleep.

"Daddy." My mom stood and kissed my forehead. She tried to hug me but it hurt. My father did the same and apologized.

"Did you know?" My mom asked and I had no idea what she was talking about.

"Know what?"

"You're making me a grandmother already Armonie. I'm too young." She smiled.

"A grandmother?"

"Let me talk to her Journey." My father said and I squeezed his hand when I tried to get comfortable. The pain was very bad.

"Ok. I'm gonna let everyone knows she's awake. I love you Armonie." She blew me a kiss and closed the door.

"I love you too mommy." I'm still a mommy and daddy's girl.

"How you feeling?" My dad sat next to me.

"Like a bunch of trucks ran over me."

"The person stabbed you four times." He pointed to the areas without lifting my gown. He also informed me of the blood vessels that popped in my eye.

"How long have I been here?"

"It happened Friday night and its Sunday. The medication had you in and out." He said and asked me to look at him.

"When did you lose it?" He inquired about something.

"Lose what?"

"Your virginity?" I shifted a little.

"I'm not comfortable talking to you about this."

"Armonie please. I broke your mothers and I'm the only man she's ever been with. I'm happy you waited as long as she did."

"She told me about you being the only man she's ever been with and I was hoping whoever my first was, it would be the same."

"Well Freddy isn't who I would've chosen to be your first."

"Freddy? No daddy, it was Ariel's cousin." He looked down at me.

"He saved me from Freddy a few times, we ran into each other at the bar and we've been around one another ever since. I wouldn't dare let Freddy touch me."

"So it's his baby and save you from what?"

"Baby?" I felt my stomach and there was a monitor on it. He pointed to a machine that I never paid attention to.

"You're twelve weeks." All the blood had to drain from my face. VJ and I never used condoms; yet it never dawned on me I could get pregnant. I didn't have any pregnancy signs and my stomach is the same.

"What am I gonna do with a baby?" I started crying.

"Well you have six months to figure it out." He kissed my forehead.

"What if he doesn't want it?"

"I'm gonna tell you like I told your mom. Your family is too big for you to worry about if a man is gonna stick around. This baby won't want for anything." Grams said when she barged in.

"My second great, great grandchild." She kissed my cheek.

"Why did he save you from Freddy?" By this time my mom, uncles, aunts, brother and a few of my cousins walked in. How did they all get here fast, but then again, they may have been waiting for me to get up.

"Where's Ariel?" I continued ignoring my father's question.

"She'll be up here tomorrow." Haven told me.

"Excuse me. It's way too many people here. I'm gonna ask everyone to leave except two." The nurse said.

"What was he saving you from Armonie?" My father badgered me with the same question.

"One second." My uncle Wolf said. They all looked at me and the pressure to speak was overwhelming.

"HE WAS BEATING ON ME OK." Its like the entire room went silent.

"I didn't tell y'all because I don't want anyone to kill him." All the men had their face turned up.

"Is that why VJ beat his ass at my club?" Haven questioned and I nodded.

"He punched me in the face and threw me against the wall. I lost consciousness for a few minutes. I woke up and Freddy was on the ground. You walked in on VJ waking me up."

"That's what he had to tell me at the restaurant and Ariel stopped him. Wait a got damn minute. Did she know?" Haven cursed.

"Yes. I begged her not to tell. She told me if I didn't say anything by today, she was telling because she was scared he'd kill me. Don't be mad at her." No one said a word.

"I don't know why I was scared to tell you. Please don't kill him. His mom is going to be hurt and..."

"And I don't give a fuck. He's a dead man walking Armonie." Colby barked and stormed out the room. My mom and aunts had tears coming down their face.

"You absolutely can not save him Armonie." My grams said and took my hand in hers.

"How many times?" My father asked. I didn't answer.

"How many times?" He asked again.

"Too many to count." I started crying and my father hugged me. Even with the pain, he made me feel safe and the weight was lifted.

"Go find Colby Jr. and handle what needs to be handled." My uncle spoke in a calm tone to Jax and Haven.

"They're gonna blame me. Please." I was hysterical crying.

"Stop crying honey. You're gonna stress the baby out." My mom climbed on the other side of the bed.

"We'll be up here tomorrow." My uncle Jax said and everyone stepped out the room but my parents and grams.

"I'm sorry daddy." He had his head back with his eyes closed.

"You should've told us." I could hear frustration and sadness in his voice.

"Who is the guy you're pregnant by?" My mother asked because she wasn't in the room when I mentioned VJ to my dad.

"He used to live down here years ago until his parents move to Virginia. I'm surprised he's not here because he was on the phone with me when I got attacked. He's very protective of me." My mom smiled and wiped my eyes.

"You love him?" I nodded and laid my head on her shoulder.

"Do you know who did this to you?" My father spoke.

"No. It was dark and after they yanked me out the car, I hit my head. I don't really remember anything but screaming for VJ to help me." I gasped.

"I have to tell him I'm ok. He probably called my cell." Grams gave me a look and my parents stared at her too.

"What?" I questioned her look.

"Nothing. You're gonna be fine. I'm sure he'll be here soon." Grams asked my dad to meet her in the hallway.

"Did you throw it on him?" My mom asked and I couldn't do anything but laugh.

"I don't know ma. He doesn't want me with anyone else and he got mad when I said he only taught me how to please him." She started cracking up.

"You may have been a virgin but if he taught you and saying that, I'd say you did."

"He's so gentle with me and he makes sure I'm done before him. I never knew making love could be that good." My mom put the covers over her legs.

"You're lucky. Some girls get the wham, bam, thank you ma'am first time sex."

"That means rough and fast right?" She shook her head yes.

"Your father taught me a lot in the bedroom but then I turned him out." I looked at her.

"On your down time always search porn sites. They have a lotta ideas a couple can use." She lifted my face.

"Explore one another regularly and switch things up. He'll appreciate it." I listened to my mom give me a sex talk.

65

My father and grams walked in asking what we were discussing. When I mentioned sex, grams tried to tell me things to do and my father covered my ears.

"She fucking now Colby. She may as well learn how to turn him out." My dad rolled his eyes. After a while, I ended up falling back to sleep shortly after.

****

"Here are your discharge papers and the prescription for your prenatal vitamins. Don't forget to follow up with a gyn doctor." The doctor said and wished me good luck.

I've been in the hospital for three days and a bitch was happy she could finally go home. Well the first two days, I was in and outta sleep but still, I didn't wanna be here. Once the results came back I was healthy, there was no need to stay any longer.

The doctor requested for me to stay a few more days but I refused. Plus, I wanted to call VJ and tell him I was ok. I hadn't heard from him and no one said a word. I don't even know where my cell phone is now that I think about it.

"Thank you." The nurse pushed me downstairs to the front door and my father helped me in the car.

"You hungry?" My mom asked and turned to me in the back seat.

"A little. Grams said she cooked for me."

"Spoiled." My dad said and drove to their house. Years ago, my father had our house built from the ground up and my grandmother has been staying there ever since.

"Like my mommy." She turned around and smiled.

"Whatever. Your mom don't run nothing."

"I don't?" She folded her arms.

"Why you always starting Monie?" Those two playfully argued all the way home. When we got there Colby Jr. was standing there with his girlfriend Jacinta who I really don't care for. She's a bitch and always complaining.

"How you doing sis?" He hugged me and walked with me to the door.

"I'm ok. I just want to eat and lay down."

"Grams been cooking since earlier. I'm sure your food is ready." He placed his hand on my stomach.

"I can't wait to have a kid. Until then I'm gonna spoil the hell out this one. I bet it's a boy."

"I want a girl."

"What does he want?" I put my head down.

"He doesn't know yet." He made me look at him.

"I may not know dude, but you trusted him enough to be your first and give you a baby. Make sure you tell him soon."

"I will." He looked at my parents and I turned around in time to see my mother shaking her head no.

"Why you shaking your head?"

"No reason. Let's eat." My mom walked in the house with my dad following like a lost puppy. When they disappeared upstairs, I knew what was up.

"Grams you didn't have to make all this." There was fried chicken, collard greens, mashed potatoes, biscuits, string beans, yams and a whole lot more. You would think it was thanksgiving.

"You're gonna have a long ride. And I'm sure you'll be there for a few days. This will hold you over." I had no clue what she was talking about.

"She doesn't know yet Grams." Colby Jr. said coming in with Jacinta on his heels.

"What y'all waiting on to tell her?"

"Tell me what?" I asked my grandmother because my brother wasn't saying anything.

"VJ is in a coma. He hasn't woken up yet."

"What? A coma?" I fell back on the chair and started crying. They explained how someone stabbed him and he may lose feeling in one arm. However; he hit his head so hard there was bleeding on the brain.

"You ok?"

"I'm fine. Colby are you taking me?" I started pulling out Tupperware to pack my plates.

"Eat first and well discuss everything else." He kissed my cheek and left me at the table. I was about to tear this food up and then go check on my man.

Ariel

"Why are you here Haven?" I woke up and he was sitting on the edge of my bed.

"You missed a lot during your beauty sleep."

"Whatever." I tossed the covers off my leg and looked at my phone. It was twelve in the afternoon. I can't believe I slept this long.

I went in the bathroom to handle my hygiene, then wrapped a bag around my arm to wash up. It was hard trying to maneuver with one limb. You never really know how much you need a body part until it's not accessible.

The soap fell on the floor and when I picked it up, Haven stood there naked. He stepped in, took the soap and helped me.

"I'm sorry." I stared at him. Never in my life of knowing him has those words ever left his mouth.

"It doesn't change anything. I walked in on you... His lips crashed on mine and before I knew it, we were in a full fledge make out session.

70

"Haven this isn't going to... got dammit." I used my good hand to grab the railing as he bent me over and assaulted my pussy from behind with his mouth.

"Here I cummmmmm." I yelled and felt my juices gushing out.

"Sexy Ariel." He smacked my ass.

"Ok now we can... FUCKKKK!" I shouted when he pushed himself inside. I was tryna say, we can talk when I get out. My pussy gripped his dick and I felt his fingertips digging in my ass. He loved squeezing it.

"I apologize Ariel. I swear it won't happen again. Mmm. You not about to keep this banging ass pussy away from me." He pounded harder and dug deeper. If I wanted to fight him off I couldn't. The euphoric feeling had me on cloud nine.

"Yea. Just like that." I threw my ass back and he caught it. I felt his hand scrunching up my hair and my body flew back to his.

"You still fucking with me Ariel?" He asked and stuck his tongue in my mouth. How did he expect me to speak?

"I don't hear you." He pulled out and pushed in so deep, I screamed.

"Say you're still fucking with me."

"Ahhhhh. Haven." He did it again and I came hard as hell.

"You want me to ask again." He swung my body around.

"You hurt me Haven. I can't keep going through this all the time. I want someone who's only for me." He lifted me up and I winced in pain because my arm hit the wall.

"You ok?" I nodded and stared down at him.

"From this moment on, I'm only for you Ariel." He plunged inside me again and my head went back.

"I swear on my parents, this is your last chance. I don't care if we're not a couple, it's only us." I popped up and down.

"Shit Ariel." His finger went in my ass and that was it. My body jerked and I could feel him twitching.

"Fuck me harder." He smiled, grabbed my waist and fucked me good and hard.

"I'm about to nut. Shit." I tried to wiggle out since we weren't using protection, but he held me tight.

"Haven I'm not on birth control." He smirked.

"I know. Fuckkkk." He came at the same time. My head was between his neck and shoulder

"Let me wash you up. We gotta be on the road soon." He let me down and handed me a towel after washing us.

"Haven you have to stop and get a pill from the pharmacy." I said walking out the bathroom.

"Not a chance."

"What?" I had my one hand on my hip.

"You're best friend pregnant. You may as well be at the same time."

"I only have one best friend and she's a virgin, which reminds me, I haven't spoken to her in a few days." My arm was in so much pain these last couple days, all I did was eat, sleep and take medicine to make the pain go away. I sat on the bed and pulled my jeans up.

"Yea well, a lot went down when you were high on drugs." I threw the pillow at him.

"Come to find out she's pregnant and guess by who?"

"Only person I can assume is Freddy. Can you button these for me?" He walked around the bed and did it for me, then helped with my shirt.

"VJ." He smirked.

"My cousin? Nah. They've never even..." I thought back to the conversation when he asked about her and how he'd grin when I mentioned her name. Then he went in her room to talk, I walk in and she was upset about something; yet neither mentioned why.

"Those sneaky motherfuckers." I laughed.

"You really didn't know?"

"Ugh no. Between me working, going to school and being under you, I didn't have time to ask or investigate. I thought he was with Mecca."

"Did you know the other nigga was beating on her?" He sat on the edge of the bed staring into space.

"Please don't tell me he got her again."

"No but somebody did. She was attacked at the hospital trying to go back and get you. She told us about it when she woke up. Why didn't you tell me?" I sat next to him.

"She begged me and Haven, I told her to tell you and Colby a bunch of times. All she was worried about is y'all killing him. She didn't want his death on her hands."

"He could've killed her."

"Which is why after the last time, I told her if she didn't say anything I was. Haven, I thought she told because I didn't hear her speaking about him anymore."

"Because she let your cousin bust it wide open. Her ass was occupied." I punched him on the arm.

"I'm serious. You had to see our face when the doctor said she was pregnant." I thought about the time I had to pull over because she threw up. She'll get worked up and vomit, but I never thought about her being pregnant because she was still a virgin. At least I thought she was.

"Was her mom mad?"

"Hell no. She wants to know why Monie making her a grandmother early." I laughed. He pushed me back on the bed and climbed on top. He was careful with my arm.

"You're my girl now." He told me instead of asking.

"I have to think about it."

"Think all you want. Ain't shit changing. It's what I say." He pressed his lips on mine and had his phone not rang, we probably would've had more sex.

"Yea. We about to pick Monie up and hit the road." Haven said.

"Nah. I'm gonna tell her on the way. A'ight see you soon." He hung up and I looked at him.

"Who is that and where are we going?"

"Where's your sneakers?" I pointed to the closet and told him which ones I wanted to wear.

"You need anything else?"

"Haven what's going on?" He helped me off the bed, walked me down the steps and straight to the car. After he started it, he looked at me.

76

"Somebody attacked your cousin. He's in a coma and there's bleeding on his brain." I broke down. He had to hold my hand in order for me to relax.

"We're picking up Armonie. Jax and Colby Jr. are coming too." I nodded and grabbed tissue out his glove box. It's gonna be a long ride.

****

"Oh my God. How is he?" I ran straight to my parents when I got in. VJ was in ICU so they were in the waiting room.

"They took him into surgery last night and stopped the bleeding. There's some swelling and they want to make sure the stab wounds don't get infected."

"Stab wounds?" Haven didn't give me the full details of VJ's attack and Armonie slept the entire ride.

"How are you Armonie?" My dad asked.

"Ok considering." She hugged him and my mom.

"Honey its only been a few days. You should be home resting." My mom told her.

"I couldn't stay home knowing he was here." I saw Monie getting ready to cry. Damn, they really were together.

77

"Are you in pain?" My mom asked.

"A lot but again, I can't sit at home. I'll rest here." The doors opened and my brother walked out with Vanity and my aunt and uncle. I gave each of them a hug.

"Aunt Maylan and uncle Vernon, this is Armonie. Armonie, this is my aunt and uncle." I introduced them.

"Damn. My son did good." My aunt smacked him.

"I'm just saying. My grand baby is gonna be cute." Armonie smiled. Brayden must've told them before we got here.

"Can I go see him?" Armonie asked and tried to keep herself from crying.

"Sure honey. He's still in the coma but he can hear you." Armonie followed and I was about to go until I noticed the way my uncle looked at Haven.

"You're the nigga who had my son jumped."

"Actually, I didn't have him jumped. He swung off, missed me and my boys fought him." Haven shrugged his shoulders.

"On your order." My uncle questioned.

78

"True but he swung first. It was fair game."

"This nigga." My uncle jumped and my father and Brayden stepped in front. Colby and Jax stood there ready.

"Stop this Vernon. It's not the time of place and he's your nieces' man." My mom chimed in.

"You still fuck with him after he jumped your cousin?" Uncle Vernon asked and I put my head down.

"Stop it. Don't you dare make her feel bad. And you got some nerve after the way you used to treat me." My mom had her hand on her hips.

"Isa." She put her hand up. My dad shook his head.

"Haven didn't know who VJ was and I'm not excusing what he did but we know my nephew can handle his own. If Maylan were out here, she'd probably curse you out for bringing it up." My uncle went back in the room.

"He's upset Haven. VJ told him a while back he was over it but that's still his son." My father told him.

"I'll be back. Try not to bring the Reaper out on anyone; especially my family." He rolled his eyes.

"I'm serious."

79

"A'ight, Ariel. Damn."

"Let me find out my sister got you in check." I turned and smirked at Brayden.

"Whatever." Haven said and waved him off. I pecked his lips and went inside with my mom.

It took a lot outta me seeing VJ laid up with machines all over. Armonie laid in the bed and had his hand on her stomach. My aunt Maylan was talking to my uncle and Vanity sat in a chair texting away.

"You ok?" I asked her.

"Yea. Antoine wants to come here but I asked him to wait." I knew her man from around the way. Well not personally but he's definitely in the streets and when she visits, he comes to the house with her.

"Why?"

"He thinks Mecca had something to do with it and wants to kill her. Shit, mommy and aunt Isa had to stop Brayden from going out there to get her." She whispered.

"Why?" She blew her breath.

"Evidently, my brother was leaving Mecca for your friend." She pointed to Armonie.

"Do you know I had no idea they were creeping?"

"From what mommy says, she knew but not the extent of how much. VJ told her he wanted to move to Jersey and when she asked why, he told her he found someone."

"Wow. I'm not gonna bother her now but I'm definitely going to ask her questions and him too."

"I want him awake now." She wiped her eyes and laid her head on my shoulder.

"I do too." I rested my head on top of hers. All we can do now is wait.

VJ

"Monie?" I whispered and rubbed her hair as she sat on the chair with her head down on the bed.

"VJ. Oh my God. You woke up." My sister jumped up screaming. Tears ran down her face as she hugged me tight.

"Vanity my arm hurts."

"You can feel it?" She asked looking down at it.

"A little. Where is everyone? What time is it?" I glanced around the room and she was the only one here. I know my parents been here and Armonie because I heard them.

"Mommy and daddy went home about two hours ago. Aunt Isa and uncle Birch went with them. Armonie..."

"She's here?" I thought my sister was her at first and when I realized she wasn't, I figured she went back to Jersey.

"She was but her mom came and had her go to the hotel."

"Why?"

"VJ she's been here since it happened. She's tired and her mom wanted her to get a good night's rest." She picked her phone up and dialed out.

"How long have I been here?" I asked.

"Three months."

"What? It felt like I slept one day." I pressed the button for a nurse to come.

"He's awake mommy." I could see Vanity crying again. She handed me the phone.

"I'm so glad you woke up. We're on our way." I looked at the time on the phone and it read 2:40 am.

"Ma, come up in the morning. It's late and I don't want y'all out."

"I love you so much son." I could hear her crying.

"I love you too ma. Tell pops I'll see him tomorrow." She blew me a kiss through the phone and hung up.

"Glad to see your awake Mr. Davis. Do you need anything before I page the doctor?" The nurse asked.

"I need to shower, shit and shave."

"VJ!" Vanity shouted.

"Vanity if I've been down that long, I need to." I turned to the nurse and asked if she could bring me a toothbrush, towels and a razor.

"I missed you brother." Vanity got in bed with me.

"I missed y'all too." I kissed her forehead.

"Did you meet Monie?" I smiled thinking about her and the fact she stayed by my side even after everything we've been through, spoke volumes.

"I did. She's very nice and overprotective as hell of you." She laughed.

"What you mean?"

"The nurses tried to wash you up and she blacked out."

"Blacked out?" I gave her the side eye.

"She told them, ain't no other woman washing her man." I laughed. I didn't even know we were a couple.

"Another time, I guess one of your flings heard what happened and tried to come visit."

"Flings? You know I didn't cheat on Mecca."

"I'm not saying you did. But this chick knew you from somewhere." She shrugged and finished telling me the story.

84

"Bro, Monie walked outside, shut it down and told her to tell anyone else who wanted to see you not to bother." I laughed harder.

"Wait until you see her."

"Why?"

"She's changed a lot since the first day we met her." I heard a machine go off and not too long after drifted off back to sleep. I guess I'll clean myself up in the morning.

****

The doctor came in around 7:30, examined me and had a tech help me in the bathroom. Well he pushed me in there and I handled my own stuff. I did have to hold on to the sink in order to get in the shower. My legs were weak from not moving but I did it.

"Hey son." My pops hugged me tight as I exited the bathroom. I heard him sniffling a little and it took him a minute to let me go.

"Let me put the break on sir and you can get in the chair." I told them I was over the bed.

"Thanks." I felt better after cleaning up. My mom hugged me tight and didn't wanna let go either. My pops had to pull her off.

"Hi everyone. I stopped to get breakfast. I hope you..." I heard Monie but her face wasn't visible yet.

"Where's VJ?" My parents stepped out the way and to say I was happy and surprised, I really was. She ran over to me, sat on my lap and placed her head in the crook of my neck. I could feel the tears on my skin.

"Let's give them a few minutes." My mom said and they stepped out the room. When she calmed down, I lifted her head and made her stand. I raised her shirt and smiled.

"When did this happen?" She chuckled and wiped her face. I thought I heard her mention a pregnancy when I was asleep, but thought it was a dream.

"Six months ago." I rubbed her belly. I had no doubt in my mind that the baby was mine.

"Damn. I wasted no time, huh?"

"I wasn't tryna trap you VJ and I didn't know until I woke up in the hospital." I pulled her back on my lap.

"What happened that night?" She started explaining and even though I was pissed over it, I was more aggravated no one knew who did it.

"Does it hurt?" I asked about the scars on her chest and side.

"Not anymore. I still have days when they do but they're far in between." I kissed each one and told her we're gonna find the person who did it. I don't want her feeling paranoid it will happen again.

"Do you know what we're having?" I wanted to know if we were having a boy. I'd love a girl, but I wanted a boy first.

"Not yet. The doctor tried to look but the baby was being rebellious and refused to turn."

"Just like his dad."

"Or her dad?" I shook my head.

"If you say so. Monie?" I turned her to look at me.

"She stabbed me because I broke up with her."

"Mecca did this?" I'm sure she was shocked like everyone else will be when they find out.

"Yes and I'm gonna get her. What I need from you is to trust me when I'm in the process of finding her."

"I don't understand." She had a confused look on her face.

"Are you my woman?"

"I think so. I mean, I kinda told everyone I was." She started laughing.

"I know we started off wrong because we both had someone. However; I will not cheat on you but I will have to come here in order to find her. I don't want you thinking bad thoughts." She nodded again and told me to do what's needed to find her.

"I missed you Monie."

"I missed you too and grams said you and Haven have to be friends now. She don't want no problems with her great, great grandbabies daddy."

"Can I make love to you Monie?" I wasn't worried about Haven and I'm positive he felt the same.

"How? You just woke up and your legs are weak."

"You're right. Let me get a quickie then. I can guarantee I'll be done fast." She tossed her head back laughing.

"Let me send your sister a message asking her to take our parents somewhere." I rubbed my hands up and down her body. Her notification went off and she showed me the message.

Vanity: *Turn him out real quick, sis in law.* I laughed and tossed her phone on the bed. She stood and took the sweats and her panties off. I lifted myself up and pulled my dick out.

"You already wet?" I rubbed her clit when she stood over me. She slid down and as good as it felt, she had pain on her face.

"It's ok Monie. Look at me." I knew she had to adjust.

"I have to get used to you again." I snatched the blanket off the bed and wrapped it around her waist. If anyone walked in, I didn't want them seeing her.

"Keep going." I moved her in circles. Her moans sounded sexy to me.

"I love you VJ." I stopped her.

89

"I was in love with you before you left." I smiled and moved her hair back.

"You told me one night I made love to you and the music was on. You tried to be low, but I heard you."

"VJ." I pulled her face close.

"I love you too Monie." I stuck my tongue in her mouth. She lifted her bottom half and rode me so good I had to hold her still because I came hard.

"I'm happy you're ok. I thought I'd have to raise the baby alone." I could hear her sniffling.

"Never." I wrapped my arms around her as she laid on my chest.

"What's that?" I moved her away.

"The baby's kicking." She put my hand on her stomach and sure enough the baby kept moving.

"Both of us had someone for years and never thought to have children with them. We meet, we fall in love and have a kid on the way." She said.

When we first met, I never thought about being with her intimately. As the days and weeks went by with me being in Jersey, we found our way to each other. I wouldn't change a thing about it either.

"I'm in love with you too Monie." I wanted to reassure her it wasn't just a loving and caring feeling. I really didn't see myself without her.

"I'm so in love with you VJ, it scares me." She and I kissed again. I know she had doubts because of how we hooked up, but I don't need to look elsewhere. She is the woman I've been waiting for.

"Let me eat real quick." I stood her up and just as I went to stick my tongue in her pussy, there was a knock on the door.

"HOLD ON!" I shouted.

Monie went in the bathroom and brought out a warm cloth to wash me. After she finished and grabbed her clothes, she went in to clean herself up. I told the person to come in.

"Oh my God. You're ok?" I couldn't get outta my seat fast enough. Who the fuck let this bitch in here?

"You think this is a game bitch?" Armonie exited the bathroom and before I could stop her, she pounced on Mecca. I mean my girl was fucking her up, pregnant and all.

"YO! Can I get some help?" I shouted for the nurse. I had no strength to break them up. The doctor finally got Monie off.

"I should've killed you." Mecca yelled and everyone looked at her. Not only did she try and kill me, but she let everyone know she's the reason I'm here.

"But you didn't. You better run bitch because there's gonna be nowhere to hide." I told her. I tried to grab the bitch by the hair to make sure she didn't get away, but my body felt weak and my head was becoming dizzy.

"Fuck you and her." I grabbed the footboard of the bed with one hand and tried to keep Monie back with the other.

"Wait a minute. You got her pregnant and not me?" Mecca tried to charge Armonie again and I pushed her back, making her fall against the wall. Blood came out the back of her head.

"Get a stretcher. Sir are you ok? Miss let me check you out." The doctor had Mecca pushed out and made Monie lie on the bed.

"Don't let that bitch leave." I was still standing there holding on to the footboard for dear life. I didn't wanna fall nor did I wanna scare Monie into thinking I wasn't ok.

"Mr. Davis please sit." The doctor said and I couldn't move.

"Just check my girl. I'm fine."

"VJ, you're sweating. Baby please sit." I could hear the worry in Monie's voice.

"What the hell happened?" Our parents ran in the room.

"How did Mecca get in here?" I asked and they all got angry.

"We went to the gift shop. She must've snuck in the room." My father grabbed my bicep and back and helped me sit in the chair.

"Is Monie ok?" I asked. My body felt worse.

"VJ I'm ok. Doctor what's wrong? Why is he sweating like that?" Is the last thing I heard before passing out. Thankfully, I was in a chair because I may not have survived another fall.

Armonie

"How you feel?" He opened his eyes and noticed we were at his house.

"I'm good. How did I get here?" He spoke quietly.

"Wellllllll. My dad heard what happened with Mecca coming in the room and had a fit because I had to beat her ass." He shook his head.

"He made some calls and had you moved right away; per me." She smiled.

"Per you?"

"Yes, per me. I'm a daddy's girl and when I mentioned the woman making me jump on her because she's the one who tried to kill you, he wasn't happy. And once you passed out, I knew then we had to remove you from the hospital."

"Wait a minute." He sat up slowly in the bed.

"I passed out, you had your dad make some calls and the doctor discharged me to come home? Do I even wanna know how he made it possible?"

"Let me give you a quick rundown of who my family is." I brought him a tooth brush and washcloth to handle his self in the bed. They didn't really want him walking around.

After he passed out, they ran various tests on him and his pressure was extremely high. They gave him some medication for the pain in his arm and crazy as it sounds, his ass slept through them moving him and me washing him up. The doctor said it was strong and he wasn't lying.

I washed him this morning and his tech we paid to come from the hospital helped me dress him after I struggled to put his boxers on. No one needed to see what he was working with, regardless if it were a man or not. His body is for my eyes only.

He handed me the hygiene stuff and said he was hungry. I sent a message to his sister and asked her to bring him lunch since breakfast was over at most places.

"Soooooooo, my dad only met my mom because his father set him up to kill her." I started telling him about my family. Its obvious we're going to be together so I may as well fill him in. Although, I didn't tell Freddy anything. Thank goodness I didn't because he would've told.

"Say what now?"

"I know. My grandfather on my father's side whose name was Freedom, had a son named Dice. Dice took over the family business because my father or my uncle Wesley didn't want to. Sadly, Dice let the power go to his head and he went to my grandparents' house on my mother side and murdered them in front of my mom and uncle Wolf."

"Damn Babe. I'm sorry."

"Thanks." I finished talking.

"My uncle Wolf witnessed the people who did it and sought revenge. He murdered Dice thinking that was the end of it. Freedom let years go by before he decided to seek revenge on Wolf."

"But he killed both of his parents." VJ said and they all thought the same thing at the time.

"Exactly. Freedom sent my father to wine and dine my mother, make her fall in love and then murder her."

"Shit." He couldn't believe it

97

"Here's where it gets complicated."

"You don't have to finish." He told me and held my hand.

"It's ok. If you're going to be in my life you should know why they're so over protective of me." He nodded.

"My father messed around and fell in love with my mother and couldn't do it. It infuriated Freedom so he sent flowers to my mom when she was pregnant and didn't expect my dad to be there. In the flowers was a small bomb that went off, causing my mom to fall and go into early labor."

"Wow."

"My father went after Freedom full speed, only to find out he had to fake his own death in order to get close. In that time, Wesley came on board when they assumed my father died. He came to my christening and attempted to rape my mom. My father was there hiding in the house and when my mother didn't come back out, he found my uncle Wesley on top of her."

"This is some shit."

"Yea. My father killed his brother and long story short, they set Freedom up and grams helped."

"Grams?"

"Yea Grams. Her and Freedom messed around years before, so she got him in her bed, did what she needed and my mom and two uncles killed Freedom in front of his remaining two kids, which are Venus and Colby.

"Your aunt and father." I nodded

"They're overprotective of me because after the explosion they thought I would die. My uncles destroyed the hospital and got arrested. From how my grams explains it, the entire situation was bad. My mom still has burns on her from the bomb."

"Y'all had a lot going on."

"I know. I'm also the first girl and evidently, I resemble my mom's mother. My uncles and mom have been super tight since birth and it's why they go hard for us."

"How did your father get me moved?"

"Oh. During the time he did hits for my grandfather, he met tons of people along the way. Politicians, cops, lawyers and so forth. My father knows a lotta people." I smiled.

"That's crazy." I gave a half smile because it really is.

"Ok, I have to know Monie."

"Know what?" I sat on his lap.

"Who's the Reaper and it better not be you." I fell out laughing. He grabbed my waist and kissed me.

"Your cousin is in love with the Reaper."

"Oh hell no." He moved me away.

"What?"

"Why Ariel? She's a good girl. What if he tries to kill her for not wanting him?" I had to laugh because he had no idea the affect Ariel had on Haven. I think it's because they knew one another for years and built a weird and crazy friendship.

"She already went through that and she's still here." I kissed his neck.

"What you mean?"

"They were creeping too and even though there was no title, they swore not to be with anyone else. She caught him with another woman and told him never to contact her again. Of course he didn't listen, went to the house and basically begged her to take him back."

"Nah. I don't believe it." He was shocked like all of us. My uncle Wolf clowned him when he found out.

"He had no choice because like you said, Ariel is a good girl and she deserves a good man. Haven wasn't tryna lose her so he had a choice to make. Her or different women. He chose her."

"He love her?" He asked.

"I say he does but he won't admit it." I grinded on his semi hard dick.

"What you tryna do?"

"Whatever you want baby." He lifted my shirt and started sucking on my chest.

"I miss you touching me." My hand was on his head.

"I miss touching you." He caressed my other breasts.

"Lift up." I did like he asked, slid my shorts to the side and gave him one hell of a ride."

"I got you when my body is better Monie." I knew he was referring to me always riding him. He wanted to make love to me and couldn't at the moment.

"Its ok babe. As long as I can get it whenever, I'll wait for you."

"You better." I laughed and ran in the bathroom to grab a washcloth and clean us up. After I finished, we were watching television when his sister walked in.

"Here y'all." Vanity burst through the door with our food.

"You gonna have to pass me a pillow Monie." I looked down and smirked at how aroused he was.

"I do that to you." I was just laying with him and here he is aroused and ready again.

"You have no idea the affect you have on me Monie. And you only have on a shirt." I leaned it to kiss him.

"A'ight y'all damn." I placed two pillows on his lap and grabbed the food.

102

"What you get me Vanity?" VJ asked and sucked his teeth. She brought him a chicken wrap that came with a soup.

"The doctor says eat light and healthy. Your blood pressure..."

"Fuck that. What you got Monie?" I opened my container and smiled.

"A burger, fries and a big piece of cake. Thanks Vanity."

"Give me some." Before I could say no, he took a huge bite out my burger.

"It feels like I haven't eaten fast food in forever." He savored the flavor.

"You not supposed to take food from pregnant people." Vanity said as I fed him some of my fries.

"Why not? I took her virginity and put the baby in her."

"Ughhh. You make me sick." I busted out laughing.

The three of us sat there joking and talking for the rest of the day. Her boyfriend Face Timed her and spoke to VJ. I loved him and his sisters' bond. It's kind of like me and Colby Jr. Haven and I are close too. You would think he was my brother at times. Now that I think of it, I'm pretty close with all the guys. We fight a lot but always have each other's back.

****

"You walking better." I told VJ who came downstairs while I was making him something to eat. He's been staying around the house since he left the hospital a couple weeks ago.

"I have to get out the bed." I turned the stove down so the food wouldn't burn and looked at him.

"What?" He asked and took a seat at the table.

"Ummm." I started fidgeting with my hands.

"Ummm, What?"

"I have a doctor's appointment in Jersey two days from now." I told him.

"Ok and."

"And as much as I love being around and taking care of you, I have to leave."

"Ok." I stopped and stared.

"You're not upset?"

"Why would I be upset Monie when I'm coming with you." A big smile plastered my face.

"You are?"

"You're about to be seven months and I missed every appointment this far. I'm not missing any more. How we getting there because you're not driving."

"Why not? VJ, I am fully capable of driving." I pouted and folded my arms.

"Monie you're tired all the time and outta 24 hours in a day, I think you sleep for 16 of them. Come over here." I walked slowly to him.

"Vanity won't have a problem driving. She already made plans to go see Antoine, so we'll catch a ride with her."

"I guess."

"You don't have to guess. It is what it is. Now finish cooking. I'm hungry and want some sex."

"We just..." He put his hand up.

"I missed three months Monie so hell yea we need to make up for lost time. Plus, after you drop my baby, you'll have to wait for sex. Therefore; you need to get used to me for good. That way after the two weeks we can have sex."

"It's six weeks VJ." I walked back to the stove.

"If you're finished bleeding in two weeks, then two weeks it is. And don't try and say you're still on it because I'm checking." I laughed at his silly ass. I think I'll be ok with him being my man for now. Especially; since he's shown me in this short time how a man is supposed to treat a woman. Even when we were creeping, he treated me way better than Freddy ever did.

Christian

"Mrs. Banks, you never signed the deed for the house, and you signed the prenup." The mediator told Elaina. The judge wanted us to see this man to get the divorce over with. If we couldn't, then it will be brought in front of him.

"Christian made me sign that stuff. I didn't have a choice." She said and I leaned over to my lawyer.

"How long are we going to be here because this dramatic scene is ridiculous?" I asked my lawyer. Elaina tried to play victim, and everyone knew it. Yet, her lawyer was still going to bat for her.

"Did he hold a gun to your head and if so, do you have it on tape? It's the only way we'd be able to corroborate your story." She put her head down when the mediator asked.

"Christian you told me I could have the house." She stared at me.

"I did before you attacked me outside the church. You do remember that right because it seems as if you're forgetting everything."

"What about your son Christian? Where's he going to live?"

"With me. Where you think?"

"Oh no. My son is staying with me." She started causing more of a scene.

"Mrs. Banks, as instructed through the courts during the restraining order process, the judge informed you that Mr. Banks will retain full custody and you are to undergo anger management classes. You are to receive two supervised visits with him per week. Did you forget?" The mediator asked.

"Christian don't take my son." I knew she loved CJ, but she also used him as a pawn to keep me around. I also know she wanted some child support.

"Elaina, you did this. I offered you the house and you declined. I offered for us to rotate with CJ weekly and you declined that as well. I even offered to pay you 10k a month in spousal support regardless of the prenup and once again, you declined. Therefore; this is how it has to be." I shrugged.

"This is ridiculous. How can a man who has murderers in his family regain custody of his son? HUH? What if they commit a murder in front of him?" She stood up talking shit.

"If I were you Elaina, I'd stop while I was ahead." I managed to get out through gritted teeth.

"Listen to him. That's a threat." She pointed to me.

"Mrs. Banks, I don't think a man telling you to stop making false accusations against his family is a threat. However; I do feel as if this isn't going anywhere. You want everything you decided to give up; including him offering you a deal on the side. I'm not sure what's going on in your head but we're not about to sit here listening to you whine like a five-year-old because you're not getting your way." I picked my phone up and sent Haven a text letting him know its ok to proceed. Its obvious Elaina thinks I'm playing.

"I want to go before a judge."

"Absolutely not." My lawyer spoke.

"We've been back and forth with Mrs. Banks and to be honest, this is just her trying to prolong the marriage so Mr. Banks can't move on with his life."

"So he can be with his whore right? Do you know he committed adultery and...?"

"I HAVE HEARD ENOUGH MRS. BANKS." The mediator shouted and slammed his pen down on the table. The old man face was beet red from being so mad.

"I am done listening to you try and tear this man down. You are acting like a spoiled brat and a courtroom or this conference room is not the place." He turned and looked at me.

"Mr. Banks, I am hereby granted the divorce and keeping the visitation in place as it stands." He looked back at Elaina.

"The divorce is final as of today and Mrs. Banks, if by some chance you decide to harass Mr. Banks, I will have you arrested for contempt, harassment and anything else I can think of to hold you." She rolled her eyes and stormed out the room.

"I apologize Mr. Banks for wasting your time." He shook my hand. I thanked my lawyer and stepped out the room with him. Brayden was sitting on a bench down the hall. If Elaina paid attention, she would've seen him. Instead she's bitching to her mother. I gave Brayden a nod and he returned the gesture letting me know things were in place.

"After you." I held the elevator for Elaina and her mother. They stepped on and I kept my eyes on the numbers lighting up.

"You should've listened." I whispered in Elaina's ear and stepped off the elevator.

"WHAT?" She shouted with an attitude. I watched Brayden step in front of me on the way down the outside stairs.

"Excuse me." She said and her eyes grew big when she noticed who it was.

"There are no excuses for dumb bitches like you." Brayden told her. He gripped her arm and once her mother tried to scream, Jerome approached her and put a gun in her back. I watched them place both women in the back of a van and pull off.

"She'll never learn." My lawyer laughed and shook my hand.

"Maybe she will now." I got in my car and headed to the place they took Elaina and her mother. I opened the door and made my way in the small warehouse. Looking at this place from the outside, you would never assume it was opened.

It was some place Haven took people to threaten them. They used Armonie's hotel to handle everything else.

I stepped inside and Elaina and her mother were on the ground crying. Brayden had chains on both of their feet just that fast. Haven did say he likes to get things done and over with.

"Christian please make them let us go." She cried. Haven strolled in with Ariel and I smiled. He seemed to be happier than I've ever seen him.

"What? Why is she here?" Elaina cried and Haven smirked.

"I'm here because none of us like you." Ariel gave her a fake smile.

"I thought it would be fun watching him torture you."

Haven snatched Elaina up by the hair and turned her upside down. Brayden connected the chains to a heavy bar hanging from the ceiling. They did her mother next. Both him and Brayden put black gloves on.

"How's your arm?" I asked Ariel who sat back with me. Haven didn't want her too close.

"If your brother wasn't getting his dick sucked and fucking some ugly bitch, my arm would be fine." Haven turned around.

"Christian don't get her started. I don't feel like fucking her til she can't walk again." Haven responded.

"YOOO! Haven stop fucking playing." Brayden shouted and we all started laughing.

"CHRISTIAN PLEASE MAKE THEM STOP!" Elaina shouted when Jerome brought in pliers, scissors and a blow torch.

"Shut up. You're even annoying when being tortured." Ariel said and I busted out laughing.

"You should hear her during sex. She'll make your dick go soft real quick." Ariel and I were cracking jokes.

"AHHHHHHH!" Elaina shouted when Jerome used the pliers to dislocate three of her fingers. Her mother passed out soon as Brayden turned on the blowtorch.

"This is Christian's last time telling you to keep your fucking mouth closed and stay away from him. Do I make myself clear?" Haven had the blowtorch on Elaina's foot.

"Yes. Please don't."

"What you think Christian? Does she mean it?" I shrugged.

"I think she'll mean it after you burn her foot off." Ariel said and we all looked at her.

"What? Make sure you do both too." She smiled and Haven shook his head. I think he was loving the way she wanted to be involved. You heard the noise from the blowtorch go on and then off.

"Get your sexy ass over here and do it." Ariel hopped up real quick and walked to him.

"Be careful with your arm." She nodded. Haven stood behind her as she almost burnt Elaina's whole foot off.

"ARIEL?" I shouted when she took the blow torch and burned all of Elaina's hair that was hanging.

"Did I do that?" She laughed.

"I'm out. Haven you and Mrs. Reaper have fun finishing up." I walked over to Elaina.

"I don't see any more problems coming from you, do I?" Elaina had passed out and I still spoke in her ear.

"Thanks bro." I hugged him, Brayden and Jerome. I never wanted to result in torturing Elaina, but she pushed me. She should be happy I didn't let them kill her.

"Bye Christian and tell Stormy, I'll call her later. I'm about to leave here and fuck…"

"Ariel you better not say it." Brayden yelled and we all started laughing.

"Just tell her I'll call tomorrow." I nodded and left them to finish up. No need for me to stick around. I'll repent at church on Sunday.

****

"I think this is it." Stormy walked out the house with a small box. We were cleaning out all Elaina's things. I put the house up for sale because I don't need any memories of my ex-wife. CJ loved staying with my grams anyway.

"You sexy when you're cleaning." I pushed the box out her hand and pulled her close.

"I'd like to think the man I'm with is the reason." She wrapped her arms around my neck.

"Oh yea." I ran my hand in the back of her pants.

"Sssss. Christian you're about to…" I slid my hand around to the front.

"I'm about to what?" I sucked on her neck when her head went back.

"I'm going to…" She stopped when we heard someone clear their throat. I snatched my hand back and stared at the detectives who must've been watching. Neither of us heard them walking up.

"Can I help you?"

"We're looking for Mr. Banks." I pushed Stormy behind me.

"For?"

"Are you him?" The other detective asked.

"Yes."

"Your wife was found on the side of the road two days ago with her mother badly burned and what looks like; tortured."

"I don't have a wife and its real disrespectful for you to say it in the presence of my woman." Stormy knew what it was but what if she didn't?

"I apologize sir. We came because you're the last person to see her at the courthouse and…" I cut him off.

"And what? We went separate ways and I haven't seen her since."

"Ok but she claims your brother and his girlfriend are the ones who attacked her." In my mind, I wanted to kill Elaina myself. I bet she thought these motherfuckers would be able to protect her but little did she know, she just fucked up.

"That's funny because my brother and his girlfriend have been in Cancun for the last week. You can check the airport records. As far as my ex-wife goes, we went through a bitter divorce and she hates me and my family right now. If anything happened to her, it has nothing to do with us. If you don't believe me, request the court records and transcripts from the mediation we went to." I stood toe to toe with one of the detectives.

"Its unfortunate what happened to the ex-Mrs. Banks, but can you remind her that the judge said any type of harassment will find her in jail."

"Mr. Banks, I know who your family is and I don't want those kind of problems. The reason we stopped by is to tell you, to let Haven know she's trying to get the FEDS involved with the case. He needs to speak with his contact over there ASAP." I shook my head laughing at Elaina.

"Also, we apologize for walking up while you were entertaining one another. We thought you heard us." I nodded. At least they weren't watching. Or maybe they were but scared to death of Haven and said they didn't.

"Thank you and I'll let Haven know when he returns from Cancun."

"Have a good night Mr. Banks." They backed away with nervous looks on their face. Had they not apologized I may have told Haven, but they seemed sorry.

I grabbed Stormy's hand and went inside to call Haven.

Elaina's gonna have to die, which means my son won't have a

mother. At this point, I can no longer save her. She made her

bed, and now has to lay in it.

Stormy

"Hey bitchhhhh. Oh my God Look how big you got." I shouted to Armonie.

She came home yesterday and called me up to have lunch with her and Ariel. I accepted the invite because after those detectives left the house, Christian was mad as hell. I've seen him upset but never outta character. When he spoke to his brother and volunteered to take Elaina out himself, I knew he had enough of her shenanigans.

I tried to calm him down with sex and it worked but he didn't sleep and was up and out early this morning. He did bring me breakfast and apologized for being in a rush. I feel sorry for his ex in a way because she wasn't catching any of the hints. I don't know what type of torture she went through, and I don't care. All I know is I don't ever wanna be the one Haven and his boys come after.

"I know right. I didn't even know I was pregnant until someone attacked me, and here I am about to give birth in two months." She and I took a seat at the table the waitress led us to.

"Where's Ariel?" I asked because she wasn't here yet.

"She worked her twelve hour shift yesterday but promised to be here." She glanced around the restaurant to see if she was here.

"How's VJ?" A grin came across her face.

"He's good. In a couple more weeks the doctor said he should be back to his normal self."

"And his arm?"

"He has feeling in it and is going to therapy, but the doctor told him, he'll have days where it will feel like the pain won't go away. Evidently, the bitch hit a few nerves." She started banging the straw on the table to get the paper off.

"It's ok Monie."

"I had that bitch Stormy. She came to his hospital room like her ass wasn't the reason he was in it. I beat the shit outta her and then she attempted to charge me. VJ threw her against the wall so hard, her head started bleeding."

"Ok. She's gone right?" I asked in a quiet voice.

"No. VJ screamed for them not to let her go but somehow the bitch ran out the hospital without being checked. She probably went to another one, but no one could find out at the time because VJ passed out and they wanted to check and make sure the baby was ok. I swear if I ever see her, I want Haven to torture her bad. I mean torture her, don't let her die, torture her some more and keep going." I don't ever wanna feel the wrath of this family.

"Well damn. My cousin must've strung you the fuck out if you sitting here tryna torture his ex." Ariel scooted in next to me. Monie said she's too big for anyone to sit by her. The waitress handed us menus and stepped off.

"How are you missy?" I asked and pointed to the hickey on her neck.

"Haven didn't want me to leave until we had sex." Me and Armonie looked at her.

"Keep it up and your ass gonna be in the same situation." She smirked.

"Bitch, you pregnant?" I shouted by accident.

"No but he damn sure trying."

"I asked you were there gonna be any little Reapers." Armonie said and we started giving our orders to the waitress.

"At the time, it wasn't an option but now that yo ass knocked up, he talking about we should be pregnant together." Ariel rolled her eyes.

"Well shit. The only one left is you." Armonie pointed to me.

"Umm not." I stared out the window for a quick second thinking about why we'll never reproduce. I have yet to tell Christian and once I do, he may not even stick around.

"You ok?" Ariel questioned and they both stared at me.

"Yea. I have a lot on my mind. Let's finish eating. I know VJ already stalking Monie." I pointed to her grinning at her screen.

"He's always hungry and not for food."

"Bitch, you got him strung out." Ariel started cracking up.

"He says no." She shrugged her shoulders.

"Yea ok." I said and we all moved away as the waitress laid our food on the table. I had to figure a way to tell Christian soon because I don't see the conversation going well if someone else tells him.

****

"You think you're better than me because your fucking my husband?" I turned to see Elaina standing there looking crazy. She wore a wig and her foot was in some brace as she held on to the crutches.

"Ex-husband." I corrected her.

"Excuse me."

"I said ex-husband." I picked up the gain laundry detergent off the shelf and placed it in my cart. Me and my mom were at Target buying things for our houses.

"Whatever. How would my ex-husband feel knowing you're sleeping around?" I stopped and looked at her.

"Oh you thought your secret was safe?" I rolled my eyes.

"You did?" She started laughing.

"I don't know what you're talking about but keep that same energy when Haven finds you again." The smile on her face faded.

"Not funny now, is it?"

"I'm not worried about Haven or anyone else."

"You shouldn't be. God didn't place us on earth to fear anyone." My mother spoke behind her.

"Mrs. Burns, I know you're not ok with your daughter sleeping with a married man." My mom looked at her.

"Stormy isn't sleeping with a married man."

"Christian is..." my mother put her hand up.

"Christian is no longer married and it doesn't matter how much you try and tell yourself it's not over, the fact remains, it is. What he does is no longer your concern."

"You're the First Lady of the church."

"Exactly and I of all people know a woman in denial when I see one." My mom pointed to her.

"Whatever. I'm going to make sure he knows your secret Stormy. Let's see if he still wants you then." She pushed her crutches forward to walk away.

125

"She knows Stormy?"

"She think she knows." My mom shook her head.

"Tell him."

"I will." We finished shopping and went to our own home.

After putting my things away, I picked my phone up and sent a message to Christian. It was killing me to do this but it has to be done.

Me: *Christian I think it's best if we go our separate ways. It's been fun and I enjoy every moment with you but it's not going to work.*

I put the phone down. A few seconds later it rang from him. I let the tears fall as he called back to back. I'd fallen for a man I can't have and regardless of how tight we were growing up, some things I kept hidden. Now I want this man and can't have him.

Haven

"I mean it Haven. You need to make peace with him before the baby shower." Grams said smoking on the back porch with me. It was our usual Sunday dinner and she was out here yelling about being friends with my cousins' man.

"Grams do you think he really gives a fuck if I talk to him or not?"

"No but Armonie will. You know she wants everyone speaking." I waved her off.

"Can I talk to Haven grams?" Armonie waddled out. Her stomach was huge for how small she is.

"What?" I blew the smoke in the opposite direction and put the blunt out.

"You and VJ don't have to speak but I don't want you two arguing around me or the baby."

"Whatever."

"I'm serious Haven. I understand the way you two met were under different circumstances but I'm your cousin and

Ariel is his. I know you don't want both of us to stop speaking to you." She folded her arms.

"I won't say shit as long as he doesn't say anything to me." I told her.

"Good. He feels the same."

"What?" I turned to look at her.

"I had this same conversation with him on the way over."

"Why you bring him here?" I asked because its only supposed to be family.

"The same reason you brought Ariel." I sucked my teeth.

"You know damn well it's different. She's always here."

"Not the point." She rested her head on my arm.

"What am I going to do with a baby?"

"Raise it."

"What if the baby's leg is like mine? You think he'll be mad and blame me?" I lifted her up.

"Uncle Colby says he loves you and I doubt he'll leave or blame you if it does happen."

"Hey y'all. Why she upset? Haven what you say?" Ariel had her hands on her hips.

"Shut yo dramatic ass up."

"I am not dramatic. You got some nerve when..." I cut her off.

"I wish you would." I know she wanted to bring up the other night when she had my ass moaning from the freaky shit she did. I ain't never had no bitch use ice on my dick. And the tricks with her tongue had me gone.

"I'm just saying." She rolled her eyes.

"Don't say shit. Ariel I'll fuck you up out here." She waved her hand.

"Anyway." She rolled her neck and flipped her hair.

"Grams said to tell y'all dinner ready and if Haven or VJ says anything smart, she stabbing both of y'all in the chest." She shrugged and went in the house. I helped Armonie up and held the door as she stepped in.

"Haven you sit there and Monie, you sit there." Grams pointed to a seat next to VJ.

"It's ok Grams. I wanna sit next to my baby daddy." Monie smiled and sat on his lap.

"You heard me chile. Now move." She shooed Armonie away.

"Um grams that was my seat." Ariel pointed to the same spot Monie tried to claim.

"Little girl don't play with me." Ariel put her hands up.

"Do I need to say it again?" I wanted to curse grams out, but I'd never hear the end of it. Plus, she'll probably shoot my ass.

"Can I sit on the other side then grams?" Monie pointed to the seat next to VJ.

"I don't care but don't let him finger pop you under the table."

"GRAMS!" My aunt Journey yelled and VJ started laughing.

"If she only knew I did more than that this morning."
VJ whispered but I heard him.

"I'm not hungry." I said.

"Haven you couldn't wait to get here to eat. Grams
made your favorite and..."

"Ariel, I swear to God you better be quiet." She thought
it was funny. I bet she won't be laughing when her ass can't
walk.

"I don't wanna sit by you either but as long as my
woman here, I'll deal with it. What I'm not gonna do is sit here
and let you pretend I'm some kind of disease."

"Fuck you nigga. We can get take it outside." I told him.

"HAVEN!" My mother shouted.

"You ain't said nothing but a word." VJ stood.
Armonie got in between us.

"Haven you're my cousin and I love you but he's my
man, my child's father and maybe husband in the future. I
can't have either of you fighting over whose ego is the
biggest."

"Monie, you ok?" He asked.

"Haven you promised not to say anything to him and you're antagonizing him for no reason. If this is how it's gonna be, we'll go. VJ can you grab my phone and purse?" He did what she asked and everyone looked at me.

"MONIE DON'T YOU DARE LEAVE." Grams shouted.

"I'm sorry grams but I refuse to allow VJ to deal with this when he hasn't done anything." VJ walked behind her and Ariel jumped in front of me with her arms folded.

"SHITTTT!" All of us heard VJ shout when he opened the door.

"Ariel can you bring me some paper towels? Monie vomited all over the floor." Again, everyone looked at me. I passed Ariel the roll of paper towels off the table and shrugged my shoulders.

"You ok honey?" My aunt Journey asked.

"I'm fine. You know how I get when I work myself up. I just wanna lay down." VJ lifted her bridal style.

"Your arm VJ. I don't want you to hurt yourself."

132

"I'm fine Monie." He walked out and I could see my aunt and Ariel cleaning up the floor. My sister Shae pushed me out the way and brought plastic bags over to them.

"You couldn't just sit there and be quiet?" My mom had her hands on her hips.

"Y'all know we don't like each other. Grams should've never tried to force us to sit by each other." I was serious. Why in the hell she thought it would be ok is beyond me.

"He's going to be around Haven and grams just wanted to make sure it would be peaceful." My mom tried to reason with me.

"No disrespect ma, but I'm a grown ass man and if I don't wanna fuck with the nigga, I don't have to."

"HOLD THE FUCK UP HAVEN!" My pops barked and it's like the entire house got quiet.

"I wouldn't care if you were 60, don't ever think it's ok to talk to my wife; your mother that way."

"It's ok Wolf." My mom stood in front of us.

"No it's not Passion." My uncle Jax chimed in and my aunt Venus tried to pull him away.

"What has gotten into you?" My mom asked.

"Nothing. I apologize if you felt like I disrespected you ma. You know I'd never do that. I stick by my word." I turned and stared at my grandmother.

"Grams should've never assumed I'd be ok with it and if y'all don't want me coming to Sunday dinner because he'll be here, I'm good. The last thing I wanna do is stress anyone out or cause harm to Armonie and the baby." I grabbed my keys and walked out the door.

"Haven." I saw Ariel running to the car with her stuff.

"How you tryna leave me when I came with you?" I unlocked the door. Both of us got in and drove off in silence.

****

"Mmmm. You feel better?" Ariel asked after sex. When we got home, we tore each other's clothes off and went at it like animals.

"Yea. You good?" She laid on top of me.

"I'm hungry." I smacked her ass.

"I am. Shit, my man left the house before we could eat." I laughed. She sat up and stared at me.

134

"I don't think you were wrong for feeling the way you did. It does seem like grams was forcing you to speak to VJ. She should've asked before trying to make y'all dinner buddies."

"Exactly!"

"However." I sucked my teeth.

"You didn't have to snap on your mom." I gave her the side eye.

"Don't you dare say, you said *no disrespect* first." I smirked.

"You came off sounding disrespectful whether you see it that way or not."

"They know how I am Ariel."

"You're right, which is why I agree to how you felt towards your grandmother doing that. It doesn't mean get mad at everyone else. Haven your mom started crying when you left and your uncles had to hold your dad. Christian couldn't even calm him down with prayer." I busted out laughing.

"I shouldn't have said that." She laughed.

"No and I'm telling Christian."

"You better not." She kept laughing.

"Well I won't go over there on Sunday's anymore."

"You're gonna break the tradition over pride? Stop it."
She moved off and went to shower.

While she was in there, I checked my phone and I had
messages from my brother, sister and cousins asking if I was
ok and to call them. Shae will curse me out and my brother and
cousins will most likely tell me I'm foul, and blah blah blah.
I'm over it. I tossed the phone on the nightstand and joined
Ariel in the shower.

Ariel

I understood how Haven felt towards his grandmother trying to get him and VJ to speak. They know like I do how Haven is and to be honest, VJ is the same. He told me the day before when I stopped by the hotel, he wasn't comfortable being around him but he'd be respectful on the strength of Monie.

I could see the anger on his face when she vomited. He wanted to say something but kept it in. He's not afraid of Haven and had Monie not said anything and left, things probably would've gotten worse.

I knew sex would relax Haven because he's an addict like me. We loved exploring one another and nothing is off limits when it comes to what we do to one another.

After we had the talk, he ordered us food, we watched a movie and fell asleep on the couch. I sure hope he gets over his attitude because their family is tight, and I don't see them having Sunday dinners without him. I mean they would, but grams wanted all of her family there and if he's not, she may cancel it.

****

"How are you?" I asked Monie when I stopped by the hotel on my way to Walmart. I wanted to pick up some things for my new house. I offered her to stay but once VJ returned to Jersey, he told her the only person she's living with is him.

"Fine. Just some Braxton Hicks here and there." I rubbed her belly. I still couldn't believe she's having a baby by my cousin.

"Where's VJ?"

"He went to check on the house with Brayden and then Virginia."

"Virginia?" I questioned and ate some bacon off the tray.

"Yea. He's packing up and moving here." I swung my body around to face her.

"Really?" She smiled.

"Yea. Do you know he said after this one he wants to get me pregnant again?" I almost choked.

138

"Talking about, lets get them out the way." She shook her head.

"Anyway, he has some movers coming here to pack me up." She was placing things in a tote.

"Pack you up?" I asked and handed her the other tray filled with food. She sat down at the table.

"The reason he went to check on the house is because they were delivering the furniture. He wanted to make sure they put everything in the right room."

"Damn y'all really about to move in with each other."

"I know right. I never thought I'd free myself of Freddy. Then VJ comes along and becomes my knight and shining armor. I give him my virginity and now it's like we're stuck like glue."

"I'd say."

KNOCK! KNOCK! We looked towards the door. She went to answer but I stopped her. She may not be with Freddy, but he still knows about this place.

I opened the door and three men stood there dressed in Cart hart jumpers. I asked for their credentials and stepped out the way as they asked Armonie where the things were she wanted moved. The things from the condo were here too. She pointed and for the next four hours we watched them move her out the hotel and into this humongous house with a big backyard and wrap around porch.

"Damn bitch. I need this bed in my life." I fell back on the bed that was bigger than a California king.

"I picked this." She used the small stepping stool to get on since it had height and climbed on.

"I would stay in here all the time. What size TV is this?" I asked because it almost took uo the whole wall.

"I think a 72 inch. Shit, it had to be big because of the room size. You can't have a 42 inch in here.

"I know that's right. You ok?" I noticed her grabbing her stomach.

"Same pains as before. When I walk too much the baby gets agitated, I guess." We started laughing. I answered the FaceTime call coming through.

"Check on Monie for me please. I keep calling and she's not answering." I could hear VJ panicking through the phone.

"Wait! Are you in my new crib?" He asked.

"First of all, hello to you too."

"Whatever. How is she?" He asked and spoke to someone wherever he was.

"Second, I want this bed and third she's having pains."

"Fuck! I told her I could wait to come here and get my stuff, but she told me she's ok. Let me call her mom."

"Oh, I'm not good enough to be here with her?"

"Cut the shit Ariel. I know you have to work but I'm glad you're there in case something goes wrong. I'm calling her mom to stay when you're gone."

"Nice save punk. Anyway, she fell asleep." I turned the phone to her.

"Ariel please stay with her until her mom comes."

"Why you so worried?" He ran his hand down his face.

"When we left Sunday dinner, she kept throwing up on the way home. I took her to the hospital, and they placed her on labor and delivery. Long story short, she was dilated two centimeters and she had some mucus leaking. She's supposed to be on bed rest or the next time she comes, they'll admit her."

"What?"

"Yea. Only you, her parents and her grams know. She didn't want anyone worrying about her."

"I'm glad you told me because she was going to Walmart with me."

"Nah she needs to stay home. Let me call her mom." He said sounded more relieved I was staying and her mom was coming.

"Ok. I'm off today but Mrs. Banks can come if she wants."

"A'ight. Thanks cuz." I could tell he appreciated me being here.

"You already know."

"Let her take a bath if she asked because it seems to relax her. Just don't leave because she'll need help getting out. And we have a lot of steps, so watch her going up and down."

"Got it. Hurry back because if she goes in labor, I'm going in the room with her mom." I stuck my tongue out and disconnected the call.

I stared at Armonie and shook my head. I made sure the downstairs door was locked, took my shoes off and fell asleep next to her.

****

"Hey you." I walked in Haven's office. Once Armonie's mom came, I talked to her for a while and decided to join my man at work.

"Why you dressed like that?" He glanced over my short dress.

"You don't like it?" I placed the food down I brought him and sat directly in front of him with my legs gapped open.

"You know I do." I leaned down to kiss him and felt his hand in between my thighs.

"We haven't fucked here yet." He said.

"And we won't." He backed away.

"You fucked your ho's here. If you wanna taste this pussy, I suggest you get a new office."

"Don't get it fucked up Ariel, if I want it, I'll take it."

"Whatever."

"But I respect it." I looked at him because the rude ass, arrogant Haven Banks had been changing right before my eyes.

"I want you to see something." He helped me off the desk and grabbed my hand.

"Oh shit now. You're holding my hand in public." I joked. He stopped and looked at me.

"Public my ass. Ain't nobody up here." I pinched him on the side. He hated that.

"A'ight Ariel." We walked out his office and into one of the other doors down the hall.

"What's this?" There was tarp on the floor, paint cans, ladders and other stuff that was covered.

"My new office." I snapped my neck.

"When Juicy died, I fucked mad bitches in the other office." I sucked my teeth.

"I'm not saying it to make you upset. I'm saying it because this club ain't going nowhere and you're my woman. I

144

couldn't have you coming here and spending time in a place others had me."

"Wow."

"It's gonna be a little while before it's finished but the window is going over there so I can still look out on the dance floor. I'm knocking down that wall to make the office a little bigger because Colby and Jax always here. They may as well have somewhere to sit."

"Why not give them an office?"

"I asked and they said no because it'll go to waste. We always in the same room so it wouldn't make sense. Plus, Jax took over his pops club and Colby opening up his own spot." He led me to another area. The room was bigger than the other and if he's breaking down walls it will be very big.

"This area over here is for you and my pain in the ass sister and cousins." He pointed to a spot on the other side of the room.

"Haven."

"I'm tryna show you I'm not going nowhere." He had me about to shed a tear.

"But you didn't have to include me."

"Why not? When yo ass running the hospital your pops building, my ass better have a spot in your office." I threw my head back laughing.

"You will baby." I draped my arms around his neck. He lifted me up and wrapped my legs around his waist.

"I better." He said.

"If I tell you something, promise you won't get mad." He looked at me.

"You pregnant?" I smiled.

"I haven't checked yet." He put me down.

"What's up?"

"Promise you won't get mad." I repeated myself.

"Say it Ariel."

"I love you. Like I'm in love with you and I'm scared you're gonna hurt me again..." He shushed me with his finger and then replaced it with a kiss.

"I love you too ma."

"You do?"

"Yea but I swear if you fuck me over like Juicy..." It was my turn to shush him with my finger.

"Never Haven. I love you too much and I don't wanna deal with you tryna kill me." I stood in front of him and pointed to my zipper.

"I'd probably do you worse because we've known one another longer. Damn." He slid the dress off my shoulder. I kept my heels on.

"I'm not worried about it because cheating isn't even in my vocabulary. But you letting me christen this room with you is."

"This is our room Ariel." He reached behind to lock the door and the two of us christened this room a few times.

Armonie

"Thanks mommy." My mother was staying with me while VJ went to VA. Oh best believe my father came too. He wasn't letting her stay anywhere without him and he wanted to make sure I was ok.

"You're welcome. A few more weeks and my first grand baby will be here."

"I know. Did daddy put the crib together?"

"Girl please. I had to stop him from breaking it." I turned to her. The crib was expensive and since VJ was in Virginia I didn't want to wait for him to come back to put it together. I wanted to have everything ready.

"Why?" I was cracking up as she told me he felt the directions were stupid and he did more cursing then actually putting it up.

"I'll be downstairs."

"Ok." She closed the door and I grabbed my pajamas. I picked the phone and answered for VJ.

"Hey babe."

"Hey. How you feeling?" He asked.

"Lonely because my man isn't here." He chuckled in the phone.

"I'll be back in a few days."

"What's taking so long?" I whined.

"Monie. I only been gone two days."

"It feels like forever." He thought I was funny.

"I'm done packing but you do remember my entire family is moving there, right?" I rolled my eyes. He decided to help all of them.

"Yes."

"Ok then. You know I'm helping them too." He reminded me.

"They don't need you tho. I do." I continued whining.

"You tryna make me feel bad?"

"No but..."

"I promise to make it up to you when I get back."

"K." I smiled.

"Look how happy you got hearing me say that." He started laughing.

"It's not my fault you got me hooked."

"I can say the same thing." I felt myself blushing. He and I stayed on the phone for a half hour.

After hanging up, I went downstairs and my mom was in the kitchen with grams cooking. I didn't even know she stopped by, but then again aunt Passion and Venus were there too, which meant my uncles were most likely in the back with my dad.

"Hey honey." My aunts hugged me.

"What are you guys doing here?"

"Oh, we can't come over?" My aunt Venus asked.

"Of course. It's just I hadn't seen or heard from anyone since the dinner." I took a seat on the couch and rested my hand on the top of my belly.

"Grams wanted to make you food and I wanted to see my niece." My aunt Passion said and handed me a small bag.

"Aunty the baby shower is in three weeks." My child didn't need a thing, but my mom wanted to have one.

"Open it." I moved the tissue paper out the way and lifted the blue Tiffany box." I opened it and gasped at the bracelet with two charms. One said, number one mom and the other was a baby with the birthstone in the middle.

"Thank you." I asked her to put it on. My aunt Venus handed me one and it too was a Tiffany's bag. I opened it and there was a necklace with my name hanging from it.

"Y'all didn't have to buy me anything." They both hugged me.

"Have you spoken to Haven?" I asked my aunt Passion because Ariel told me what happened after we left.

"Yea. He stopped by to apologize like the brat he is." She smiled.

"What about uncle Wolf?"

"You know he ripped him a new asshole and then they went to smoke." She rolled her eyes.

"Have you spoken to him?" My mom strolled in with Grams.

"No. I'm ok though." They all looked at me.

"Him and VJ never have to speak and I understand why he was upset about grams trying to make them. But he stood there talking shit to VJ the entire time; well indirectly anyway."

"I'm not excusing him but we all know the type of person Haven is. Just know they may not ever speak but it shouldn't stop you from attending dinner." My aunt Passion said.

"I'm not going to come without VJ and I don't want them fighting." I started crying.

"Stop crying." Grams said and took my hands in hers.

"The way they met were under bad circumstances and both of them have to get over themselves." I looked at grams.

"Both of them Armonie."

"Grams, Haven started with him both times. Is it fair to ask VJ to let it go?" They all looked at me.

"Exactly! I love my cousin but he's my man and I have to keep them away from each other."

"I can't argue with that." Grams said and went in the kitchen to check the food. Everyone wanted peace just like I did. However; I'd never ask VJ to speak to my cousin after all the things that have gone down.

Four hours went by and after eating and joking around with everyone, I was tired. The clock read ten and my body surely felt it. I gave all them a hug, a kiss goodbye and retreated upstairs after helping them clean up. Or should I say watch because none of them let me do anything.

"Hey." My dad walked in my room and laid on the bed with me.

"Hey."

"Did I ever tell you the story about me and your two uncles who just left?" He asked.

"No." I never knew they didn't speak and none of them brought it up. You would think they'd been cool forever.

"Well I didn't know them in the beginning and when we did meet, it was at the hospital after my father had Wolf shot."

"Really?"

"Yup. I had just confessed to cheating on your mom the day before and tryna get her to take me back."

"You cheated on mommy?" I was learning a lotta new stuff.

"Yes but only because my ex was blackmailing me. She knew the true purpose of why I dated your mom. Instead of telling my future wife, I slept with her to keep quiet." I turned my face up.

"You look just like your mom making that face." I didn't say anything

"Anyway, the following day your mom told me who murdered her parents and it all hit me on why my father put a hit on her. She received a phone call from your aunt Passion about your uncle getting shot, right after. When we got there, I still had no clue who he was until Wesley stormed in yelling about killing the guy who shot our brother."

"Interesting." I said.

"Oh it was. Long story short, me and your mom stayed together but I didn't fuck with her brothers and she never asked me. We got into a lot of arguments, Wolf and I shot one another and it wasn't until you and your mom almost died, and I had to bail them outta jail, did we speak. Even then it was kinda strained."

"Wow daddy."

"In the end, we all had one thing in common which was killing my father."

"Oh." He made me look at him.

"I'm telling you this to say, VJ and Haven may never speak and that's fine. As long as they both have your best interest at heart and protect you at all cost, their friendship don't matter."

"But I want them to be friend's daddy."

"You can't force a friendship on men. They have egos and their pride. If it's something they wanna do, let it happen on its own." He stood up and kissed my forehead.

"Thanks."

"Anytime. Now let me go help your mother sleep good."

"Ughhhh." He laughed and closed the door on the way out. I grabbed the phone and FaceTime'd VJ.

"You ready for bed?" He answered lying down in the hotel room. He could've stayed at his parents, but he said his mom was driving him crazy about his arm and the whole situation altogether.

"Where are your clothes mister?" I smiled staring at his bare chest.

"My girl likes when I sleep naked."

"Yea well your girl not there." He laughed.

"Nah but she'll be next to me soon enough. Let me see my son." He asked me to show him my belly.

"VJ the baby could be a girl."

"Nope." I shook my head and lifted my shirt for him to see.

"I'll be home in a few days son. Keep your mommy safe." I felt him kick my stomach.

"Ok babe. I'm putting the charger on and the phone on the nightstand." Since he's been gone, he had me sleeping with FaceTime on so he can watch me. If anything happens, he could call my parents.

"Love you Monie." I always smiled when he said it.

"Love you too. Hurry home." I blew him a kiss and waited for sleep to find me.

****

"GUESS WHAT BITCH!" Ariel barge in my room shouting.

"Yo! Why the fuck you wake her up?" VJ barked in the phone.

"What the hell? You two are losers." She picked the phone up and started talking shit to him. I flipped the covers and went to wash my face and get it together.

"Tell Monie to call me when you leave." I heard VJ say.

"Ok babe." I yelled from the bathroom.

"Bitch, Haven told me he loved me and I think he got me pregnant last night too." I spit my toothpaste out.

"Girl he's even changing his club around to make sure I know it's all about me."

"Awww Ariel. I'm so happy for you." I cleaned my mouth and stepped out.

"Have you mentioned the reason you weren't getting pregnant?" Ariel had the depo shot right before her and Haven started sleeping together. She knew they were careful, so she never went back to get the new shot when it was due. It's been a few months and she's not pregnant, which eventually he's gonna wonder.

"Hell no bitch. Are you crazy?" I turned to her.

"I'm almost due Ariel and he's gonna ask questions. Tell him before he starts thinking he can't have kids."

"We had a good night so maybe tomorrow. What you doing today?" She asked knowing I shouldn't leave the house.

"Not a damn thing."

"Are you allowed to go to the salon because bitch you look a mess. Don't be slacking now since VJ's your man."

"Whatever. Let me call aunt Venus and see if she can fit us in. I do need a fill in and my feet done."

"And this head." She flipped my hair. I called my aunt and she said we could come.

I went to the room my parents stayed in and turned around when my dad moaned out my mother's name.

"Your mom coming?" Ariel asked flipping through channels.

"I doubt it. She turning my dad out."

"Ok Mrs. Banks." We laughed and I prepared myself to go out. I sent my mom and VJ a text where I was going. I need this fresh air.

VJ

"You ready?" Brayden asked. We were on our way to Mecca's sister house to see if she's there. I didn't tell Monie because she'd worry.

"Yup."

I had Brayden drive the rent a car because I'm not sure what my ex told them. If they saw me coming, they probably wouldn't open the door.

All I could think about is killing Mecca with my bare hands. I understand she was upset but stabbing me is where she fucked up. Vanity wanted to come but Antoine was here and not allowing it. He said she runs a business and didn't need to associate herself with street shit.

Brayden parked in front of the house. Me, Mycah, Brayden and Antoine stepped out. Because she lived in the hood, bitches were everywhere and I couldn't help but notice one in particular. Lily made eye contact and headed towards us. Brayden asked who she was and changed his mind about tryna fuck after I told him she for everybody.

"Hey VJ. I'm happy to hear you're ok. When Mecca called and said someone tried to kill you, we were all worried the person would come back for her."

"We?" I questioned and never responded to her assuming it wasn't Mecca.

"Yea, me, her mom and sister."

"Where Mecca now?"

"I haven't seen her since she moved." I could tell she was lying. That's her best friend and I know Mecca has contacted her.

"Moved? Why would she move?"

"She said y'all broke up and..." I yoked Lily up by her hair. If the bitch knew we broke up, then Mecca told her.

"Where is she?"

"VJ let go."

CLICK! I pulled the gun from my waist and put it under her chin.

"Where the fuck is she?" Lily started crying.

"I swear I don't know. I haven't spoken to her since that night." I pushed her off.

"When I find her because I will, I'm not gonna have any mercy on her."

"Y'all have years in tho. Whatever she did, why can't you forgive her?" Slowly but surely Lily was telling on herself.

"What she did can't be forgiven and if I find out you had something to do with where she is, I'm gonna have my cousin cut your tongue out for lying before he kills you."

"I...I... don't know where she is." The stuttering gave her away.

"Sure you don't. Let Mecca know she can't hide, and I will find her." We all got in the car to leave. It wasn't a need for me to ask her sister because it's clear Lily knows exactly where she is.

"What you wanna do?" I glanced down at my phone for the second time at the text Monie sent me. She's having more and more pain everyday. The doctor said the baby's getting ready for his arrival.

"I'll return after Monie has the baby. She's too close and I don't wanna risk missing the birth. She'll never forgive me and I'll never forgive myself."

162

"A'ight." Brayden pulled off and I stared Lily dead in her face. She can think I'm playing if she wants. I do know she's gonna relay that message and I have no doubt Mecca will slip up.

****

When I walked in the house Monie's parents were just going to bed. Her mom hugged me, and her pops said he wanted to talk later. No idea about what but it has to wait because Monie's doctors wanted to see her every two weeks since she came in after the dinner.

"Mmmmm baby. I missed you. Sssss." Monie moaned out when I sucked in between her thighs and latched on to her clit. She assumed I was returning tomorrow but we were all done in VA, so it wasn't a need to stay longer.

"Show me how much." I looked up. Her back was arch, she held on to the sheets tight and once my finger went inside, she let herself go. I missed tasting her, so I continued to give her a few more.

"I missed you too." I kissed up her legs, then her stomach and found her mouth.

"Can you hang?" I let the top of my dick run up and down her slit. She bit down on her lip and I almost came from how sexy it was.

"Tell me if it hurts." She nodded and accepted me in. Her pussy gripped my dick so tight I came right away.

"Shit." I leaned on the side of her because I didn't wanna lay on her stomach.

"It's ok. Stand up." She told me.

"Huh."

"Stand up." I got off the bed, stood and helped her sit up.

"Monie, I could've waited until... oh damn." Her two hands were on my ass while she sucked me back to life.

"I promise to swallow next time VJ. I just want to feel you right now."

"You don't always have to swallow Monie." I lifted her face.

"I'll never question if you don't and I want the same thing right now." I had her get on all fours, entered my favorite place and enjoyed myself for the next hour.

"You hungry?" Monie asked as I cleaned us up.

"No. Let me get some rest and we can go out to breakfast if you want.

"As long as you're here, we can stay in." She snuggled underneath me, placed my arm on her belly and both of us were out.

By the time we woke up, it was after twelve.

"Ummm, so I don't think we should go to the doctor." Monie yelled but not too loud from the bedroom. I was brushing my teeth.

"Why not?" I shouted the best I could with toothpaste in my mouth.

"MAAAAAA." She shouted, which made me run out.

"What's wrong?"

"You have toothpaste sliding down your mouth." She joked but pain was all over face.

"Who cares? What's wrong?" Her parents ran in the room.

"You ok?" She wasn't talking and tears were falling down her face.

"Oh my God. Your water broke." Her mom said. Me and her father looked, and sure enough Monie's sweats were wet.

"Fuck!" I ran in the bathroom, cleaned my face and ran back in the room.

"Are you in pain?" Her mom asked and she said just a little but her facial expressions said different.

"I need to change. VJ can you wash me up real quick?"

"Ok. We'll be downstairs waiting for you." Her dad kissed her forehead, while her mom couldn't stop smiling. I washed and changed her clothes before helping her down the stairs.

"Where's the baby bag?" Her mom had it on her shoulder.

"Off to the hospital we go." I held Monie's hand the entire way. Her parents kept asking if she were contracting. I picked my phone up to call my family.

"VJ, I think one of your boxes is here." My mom said answering.

"Ma, Monie's in labor. Her water broke."

"WHAT?" I could hear her yelling to everyone at the house.

"We'll be there. Tell Monie congratulations on becoming a mommy." I smiled and looked at her taking breaths.

"I will." I hung up and sent a text to Brayden and Vanity. I know she's with Antoine and he's probably with his girl. I almost forgot to send one to Ariel. She would've had a fit.

"Here we go." I said when her dad pulled into the hospital. I went in and asked for a wheelchair. The nurse came out and helped put her in one and then it started.

"AHHHHHH!" Monie yelled and squeezed the hell outta my hand. It's like the baby knew we were at the hospital because that's when the contractions really kicked in.

"VJ it hurts." I stood there watching her facial expressions and tryna calm her down. I don't know how she's doing it but I respect the he'll outta women for this.

"Ok. We need to get her in a gown and on the bed." The nurse said and we both helped Monie out the chair. After she had the gown on, the nurse hooked different monitors up and put one on her belly. You could hear my kids' heartbeat right away.

"Oh shit. We about to have a baby." Ariel strolled in.

"What the hell you doing here?" She pointed to her scrubs.

"Did you tell everyone?" I heard Monie ask and kept my comments to myself. They're a tight family so I'm sure she wants all of them here. Ariel looked at me and I nodded.

"I sent him a text. VJ look." She tried to speak and I cut her off.

"I don't wanna discuss him or nobody else right now. My girl about to have my baby and it's the only thing I'm focused on." Her dad smirked and Monie squeezed my hand when another contraction hit.

After twelve hours of labor Monie finally pushed my son out. I was happy as hell and so was her dad. The delivery took a toll on Monie too. They gave her some pain medication that put her straight to sleep.

"Where's my cousin?" Haven stepped in the room with some balloons. Everyone looked from me to him. I had my son in my arms and placed him back in the bassinet.

"I'll be back." I went to walk out and I saw Monie's dad stand in between us. I wasn't leaving because he came per say. I left because he had every right to see my son and Monie would cuss me out if I made a scene. Therefore; the best thing for me was to make an exit.

"Can I smoke with you?" I heard Colby Jr say. Him, Jax and Brayden were behind me.

"Who said I'm smoking?" I pressed the elevator button.

"My cousin stepped in and you stepped out. Anyone can see you need a smoke." Jax said and pulled a blunt from behind his ear.

"That obvious huh?"

"Ugh Yea." Him and Colby Jr laughed. I didn't have a problem with them. They spoke when we were around one another, and none of us were disrespectful to the other.

We stepped on the elevator and made our way outside to one of their cars.

"Sooo, what you naming him?" Colby asked.

"Legend. It's too many V's in my family." Jax nodded.

"I don't think I'm gonna name my son after me either. After a while, shit gets confusing on who you talking too." Brayden shrugged his shoulders after saying it.

"Did anyone find Freddy?" I asked passing the blunt. Jax had one too but we sparked both of them.

"After we found out he was beating Armonie, we ran down on his crib and his parents." Colby answered.

"Good."

"He wasn't at either place. After Haven beat up his pops to try and find his whereabouts, it's like the entire family disappeared but the mother. I mean they don't live there anymore but the mama goes to church faithfully." Jax said.

"We followed her home a few times and she's staying with her sister." Colby chimed in.

"It's all good. I'm gonna find him and instead of beating him down like usual, I'm gonna kill him." They both turned around to me.

"So my sister got you killing for her already?" He had a smirk on his face.

"I'll kill for her and my son now and I'm not even a street nigga."

"We know." Both of them shouted.

"What?"

"That day at the restaurant, Haven sent me a photo of you and let's just say we knew who you were a long time ago. We didn't know you were with my sister because y'all kept that shit on the low but we know the rest."

"Why am I not surprised?" I sucked my teeth.

"You and Haven are more alike than you think." Jax blew smoke in the air.

"Doubt it."

"I'm serious. Y'all both love Monie and Ariel. Both of y'all won't stand down or move your pride to the side and have bad ass tempers."

"Whatever." I waved Colby off.

"See. Y'all answers are even the same." I looked at them.

"Oh, you think we didn't say nothing about that petty shit he did at Grams? Nah, we dug in his ass too. One thing we don't play is disrespect and whether he fucked with you or not, you were Monie's guest. Never once has Armonie left a dinner until that day, which upset everyone." Jax said.

"Grams is getting old, and we never know when she'll take her last breath, so we try and make it there every week. When Monie left, I think it's the first time I've seen her cry in a long time, besides when Christian's dumb ex-wife had CJ, and today when my sister had your son."

"I didn't have a problem staying but you're right, I was Monie's guest so when she was ready, I left with her."

"Look. Y'all ain't never gotta be friends. All we ask is for y'all be cordial." I nodded.

"We know you defended yourself at Grams so don't think we tryna say you shouldn't have." Colby said.

"Nah I get it. The nigga not welcomed at our house but I'll never ask Armonie to keep my son from around him. He's with my cousin and it would be hard anyway. I'm just not gonna pretend he can sit up in my house."

"I respect it. Shit, I'd be saying the same thing." We sat out there a little while longer. When we walked back in, everyone was still in there.

I sat outside the room checking emails on my phone, along with making sure the financial part of the business was up to par. After they all left, I stepped in the room.

"Hey baby. Where'd you go?" Monie asked feeding Legend. I closed the door, took my shoes off, washed my hands and got in bed with her.

"I gave your family time to be with you." I kissed her forehead.

"I love you VJ and whether you speak to him or not, my feelings won't change."

"I know. I love you too and thanks for giving me my son." She handed me the burp cloth and then my son.

"Goodnight babe." She turned over a little and I watched her and my son sleep until I drifted off myself.

Mecca

"Bitch your nigga tried to kill me." Lily shouted when she barged in Raheem's house. He went out to get some food. I sat up on the bed and stared at her.

"Why would Raheem try and kill you?"

"Bitch don't play with me. You know damn well I'm talking about VJ." She slammed her purse on the dresser.

"What the fuck happened between you two?" I rested my head on the pillow. I never told her or Raheem the truth.

"Fine. He broke up with me and I stabbed him."

"YOU DID WHAT?" She shouted.

"Do you know he almost killed me looking for you?"

"Why would he try and kill you?" I got out the bed and went to the bathroom.

"He thinks I know where you are?" I stopped and turned.

"You didn't tell him, did you?" I asked nervously. She was so mad, it's no telling if she did or not.

"No but I should've. He told me his cousin his gonna cut my tongue out before he kills me if they find out I knew where you were." I waved her off and closed the bathroom door. Is he really searching for me?

BANG! BANG!

"Hold on Lily."

"Hurry up because we need to discuss this." I used the bathroom, washed my hands and opened the door.

BAM! This bitch punched me dead in the face. I stumbled back and thought about hitting her but my ass ain't fucking with her or no levels. She takes up boxing too. I'll let her get that.

"What the hell you doing Lily?" I heard the door slam as blood poured out my nose and she continued hitting me.

"Let go." She held my hair and got a few more hits before he pulled her off.

"She gotta go." Raheem helped me off the floor and had me sit on the toilet with tissue. He tilted my head back and told me to stay put.

"Why you hitting her?"

"Raheem all this time she had us thinking someone stabbed VJ when she's the one who did it. Then he threatens me over her and I'm not about to let you lose your life over her."

"Why would I lose my life?" Was Raheem that stupid? Even I knew what she meant.

"Whoever has her is going to die. His cousin came from Jersey and from what I hear, he's best friends with some guy named the Reaper. I know you heard the stories about them because the whole world probably did." She went on and on.

"What she talking about Mecca? Is he looking for you and why didn't you tell me? You know that nigga ain't feeling me since he found out about us." I remained quiet. He's right.

When VJ found out about us, we were in Jersey. Mycah came running his mouth and things went downhill from there. It makes me wonder if Mycah never ran his mouth would we still be together. Then he went and got the other bitch pregnant which is a slap in my face. He's never even fucked me without a condom.

"He's not looking for you. And yes, I stabbed him and ran." I decided to leave out how I showed up at the hospital.

After the bitch whooped my ass and he threw me into the wall, I came to and hauled ass out the hospital. If she were there, it meant other family members were too and I couldn't take the chance of getting caught.

I stayed at my moms for a few days and told her I was jumped at the mall because VJ cheated and the girl found me. Say what you want but I couldn't tell her the truth. She'd be the first to tell him where I was. We don't see eye to eye, and I haven't lived with her since I graduated high school.

"Why?"

"Because he broke up with her stupid ass."

"Fuck you Lily." I could talk shit because Raheem wouldn't let her touch me.

"Fuck me?" She moved closer and Raheem stepped in front of her like I knew he would.

"What's crazy is you had a good man. A man any woman would love to be with but yo ho ass had to dip out because he was working."

"Really Lily?" Raheem questioned.

"Hell yea really. This bitch had me tryna fuck VJ any chance I could just to see if he'd be with it and he never was. He shut bitches down at the strip club for tryna fuck because he didn't wanna lose Mecca and what did she do? She cheated and then stabbed him because he didn't want her no more." Raheem turned to me and I had tears rolling down my face.

Lily was absolutely right. VJ didn't cheat on me and I thought sending her would make him because she's gorgeous. Every time she told me no, I'd ask her to try again. I don't know if it was my conscience because of what I did with Raheem or what. Then, I stab him for no reason and now he's searching all over for me.

"Why didn't you just leave him?" I removed the tissue and walked back in the bathroom to clean my face. Blood was all over my hands and clothes.

"SHE HAS TO GO RAHEEM. I'M NOT TRYNA DIE OR LOSE MY FAVORITE COUSIN." I heard her shout when I started the shower.

"I'll talk to you later Lily." I heard the door slam and stepped in. I could see the blood on the ground and shook my head.

"You're gonna be fine." Raheem stepped in.

"Maybe I should leave. I don't want you to get hurt." He turned me to face him.

"I'm not and we're gonna make him pay for hurting you and threatening my cousin." I looked at him.

"Don't worry yourself with how. Just know he's gonna get what's coming to him." I don't know why but a smile graced my face.

"You know I love you girl."

"I love you too." We started kissing and took it to the bedroom where he had me screaming his name. In my opinion VJ is still better but I'll take this.

****

"Mecca said there's a safe inside the main building. It's where they keep the money from the tenants." I heard Raheem talking to someone in the living room. I peeked out and there sat two guys I've seen around the hood. They speak to VJ when we out, but I had no clue either of them would be down to rob him. To be honest, I thought Raheem was going in alone.

Yep, I sure did tell him about the safe. I've been to the office so many times and saw the transactions. If he were in a different building, he'd collect the money and take it to the safe if the banks were closed. I told him the best time to rob him is now, because it's the beginning of the month. It means everyone was paying their rent so the money will be there.

"You sure about this?" One of the guys asked.

"Hell yea. The whole family moved to Jersey. There's a management team maintaining the building but what they gonna do?" Raheem told them.

"A'ight because I'm not tryna die." The same guy said in a nervous tone.

"Nigga did you not hear me say the whole family in Jersey? Plus, that nigga just had a baby. He ain't coming here." My heart shattered in a million pieces when Raheem blurted it out. I knew she was pregnant and maybe I was in denial, but how could he? At this point I hope they take anything they see.

Haven

"Tha fuck you want Marlena?" I walked past her outside the club. I hadn't seen her in a while and I damn sure wasn't looking for her.

"Are you really dissing me for some whack ass nurse?" I stopped and turned around.

"Who told you that?" One thing I didn't like is for outsiders to know my business. I'm not confirming anything to her but I still wanna know who told her.

"Duhhhh!" She opened her phone and showed me a picture Ariel took of us yesterday when she went to pick her graduation stuff up. It said future RN and hubby under the caption. I smiled a little because she had my ass stuck.

"Why you following my girl?" I walked in the club and noticed Sharika sitting at the bar. Why is she here? To my knowledge she doesn't go out or at least come here.

"Her page is open and why not? I need to know whose ass I'm gonna beat." I snapped my neck and looked at her.

"Whose what?" I moved closer. She swallowed hard and I nodded for security to come get her.

"I'm saying Haven. I made a lotta money stripping and fucking you. That bitch comes in and now I'm no longer allowed upstairs. When you and Juicy were together it didn't stop you. You don't give me money or...." I pushed her to the side door with security behind me.

"You made yourself sound like a prostitute and if that's what you're calling yourself so be it. But you fucked up disrespecting my girl and my club with your bullshit."

"Haven..."

"You're fired."

"What?" I hate when you're standing in someone's face and they pretend not to hear what you said.

"You heard me. You're fired. Bring your ass back in here and I promise you won't make it outta here alive." I opened the door and threw her out. She hit the ground hard as hell.

"I don't wanna see her in here again." Security nodded and I went to where Sharika sat.

"What are you doing here?"

"I came to see you." I gave her the side eye. She's another one I haven't seen.

"About?"

"Can we speak in private?" I looked around and went to the foyer area by the front door. Ariel be popping up now and I don't want no problems.

"What's up?" She glanced around.

"Here?"

"Yes here. My girl will flip the hell out if I take a woman in my office." She folded her arms.

"Is she the reason I haven't seen you?" Is this bitch dumb? Maybe that's why her baby daddy told her to get rid of the kids.

"Ugh Yea. What you think this is?"

"I miss you Haven and when Juicy was here..." I cut her off.

"Why does everyone keep bringing up my ex?"

"I don't know about the other chicks but when y'all were together, so were we. As long as I kept my mouth closed it was all good."

"Yea, well this one ain't having it. Matter of fact, you should back away." I surveyed the front door and behind me to make sure Ariel wasn't lurking.

"It's like that?

"Just like that? Anything else?" She put her head down.

"The job wouldn't let me transfer and I'm only part time because it's slow."

"Bitch, how the post office slow?"

"My boss is mad I wanted to transfer and started shorting me hours. I can't prove what she saying is a lie, so I have to take what she offers?"

"You tryna strip or something?" I looked her up and down.

"Heck no." She shouted and turned to see if anyone was paying attention.

"Oh, because I was gonna say your body ain't up to par for the niggas who frequent here."

184

"Excuse me." She put her hands on her hips and caught an attitude.

"I'm just saying your tities droop a little, your ass is a tad bit flat and working here men may wanna take you home afterwards." Her mouth hit the floor.

"I'm not saying you had to, but I know what the pussy like and it's just ok. Your head game may bring in some money but..."

"Oh my God Haven can you be any ruder?"

"Oh, you want me to finish?"

"No. I think you said enough." Her eyes began to water.

"What you want then?"

"Can you give me some money like the last time?" She put her head down after asking.

"Are you serious? I gave yo ass five thousand dollars. I know it was a while back but you're telling me you didn't put it in the bank? Where is it?" She became embarrassed.

"Don't shut down now. Where is it?"

"I sent it to my mom because it was going to an apartment in Texas." I didn't know if I should believe her or not.

"Tell her to send it back."

"I tried but she won't."

"Man here." I took the two grand I had and handed it to her.

"Don't ask me for shit else. The boy has a father. Get over your pride and off that high horse and call him. Shit, if he buying his girl a house, he got it."

"I'm not asking him for anything."

"That's on you but make this your last time you ask me. I'm not your man or baby daddy." She nodded, attempted to hug me until I pushed her off and walked out. These bitches are crazy.

****

"I'm going to see Legend today. You coming?" Ariel asked coming out the bedroom.

"I'm good. Tell grams to send me a plate."

"HAVEN BANKS STOP THIS SHIT! YOU'VE MISSED A LOT OF DINNERS AND ITS AFFECTING YOUR FAMILY." I looked up from the living room television.

"Who you tryna boss up on?"

"You Haven. This is ridiculous and you know it. Will VJ be there? Yes, but stay away from him and grams definitely won't try and put y'all together. Everyone misses you; especially Armonie." I sucked my teeth.

"Then your brother going through it because Stormy not only left him but hasn't been to church."

"What?"

"She broke up with him through a text message your mom said. Haven, he was there for you when the reaper handled Juicy. He needs someone to talk to."

"He has everyone else."

"I SWEAR TO GOD IF YOU DON'T PUT SOME CLOTHES ON, I'M NOT GIVING YOU ANY UNTIL YOU ATTEND A SUNDAY DINNER."

"Lies." I joked and she stood in front of me looking like she's about to cry.

"Damn, it took you forever to get pregnant."

"Excuse me!" Her hands were folded across her chest.

"I've been letting off in you forever and it wasn't until today that I can tell you are."

"Haven I haven't taken a test and..." I stood and shushed her with my finger.

"A nigga knows when his woman pussy changes." I left her standing there speechless and went up to the bedroom.

"Ummm. Are you coming?" She leaned on the door not knowing what to say.

"I'm only going because you're not supposed to turn a pregnant woman down."

"We don't even know if I am."

"Don't you worry. Grams has tests and she'll have no problem giving you one." She rolled her eyes.

"I love you Haven, and I hate what's going on with you and my cousin. Please don't get over here and make a scene." She started tearing up again.

"There you go about to cry again." I walked over putting my jeans on and watched her lay back on the bed.

"I love you too Ariel and be happy you're pregnant because I was about to ask questions." She gave me a crazy look.

"I may be a lotta things but stupid ain't one of them." Now she was scared.

"Whatever you did or were doing not to get pregnant better not ever come out if its bad." She went to speak again.

"I don't wanna hear excuses. You're about to be my child's mother but don't get it twisted. I'll still kill you if I find out you've been murdering my kids." I kissed her forehead and backed away to finish getting dressed. Ariel was so scared, she didn't move.

"I wonder what grams is cooking and don't call because I wanna surprise her." Still sitting there stuck, Ariel took a few more minutes before getting up.

I wasn't tryna scare her because it's not something I ever wanna do to her. But my cousin was three months when I started cumming in Ariel. It might not have happened the first day, but we haven't worn a condom since, and I've just started feeling the difference in her pussy a few weeks ago. I'd hate to

189

kill her for getting an abortion or even taking those plan b pills. She knew the risks like I did and never told me to pull out.

I don't know if I'm having those thoughts because of what Sharika went through or what. All I know is, Ariel better have a good ass reason on why she's recently pregnant.

"I'm ready." I grabbed her hand in mine and led her downstairs and to the car.

"You hungry?" I asked.

"Yea."

"Good. Let's go." I started the car and pulled off in route to grams. This is gonna be fun.

Ariel

Haven drove to grams house smiling and talking about how he thought he'd never have kids. Evidently, Juicy didn't want any because of the transformation Haven paid for her to have. She didn't want a baby to mess up her body. However, she messed around and cheated on him and we all know what happened to her.

Anyway, he did scare me when he mentioned taking my life if I aborted his kids. I didn't take any plan b pills or go to a clinic. The depo shot really had my body take its time in getting pregnant.

I'll tell him later because right now we're pulling up to grams and everybody car is here; including the new Tesla truck VJ purchased Armonie for a push gift. I really loved their relationship and he seems a lot happier with her.

"Whose Tesla is this? This shit fire." Haven asked looking at it.

"My cousin brought it for Armonie."

"For what? It's not her birthday." He tried to look inside.

"It's called a push gift. It's because she had his son."

"Oh. I ain't buying you no truck when you push out my kid." He is so fucking ignorant, but my ass can't seem to leave him alone.

"Whatever." He took my hand in his as we walked through the door. Everybody was sitting at the table and some in the living room.

"Haven you came." His mom said which made everyone turn around.

"I had to. Grams act like she can't send me no food."

"And I wasn't nigga. You holding out on my shit." I busted out laughing and told her I had it. She wanted her weed I brought every Sunday.

"Oh. Ariel needs to take a test."

"REALLY!" His mom rushed over, grabbed my hand and took me in the bathroom.

"You do know he's going to put more babies in you? Haven wants at least eight kids." His mom said making me laugh.

"Maybe two or three but eight. I don't think so." I asked her to give me a minute to use the bathroom. As soon as I pulled my pants and panties down, Haven barged right in.

"Damn babe. Can I piss on my own?"

"I wanna make sure you don't put water on the test to make it say you're not. Or use somebody else pee to say you are." What is wrong with this man? He was dead serious.

"You're a fucking nut. Pass me the test so I can go." I was holding it in.

"Here."

"Open it without touching the inside." I told him.

"You bugging." He handed it to me unopened. I took the paper off, slid it in between my legs and went to the bathroom. I took some tissue off the roll and sat the test on top of it.

"How long?" He asked

"Read the box Haven." I wiped, pulled my clothes up and washed my hands.

"Where you going?" He reached for my hand.

"I'm hungry Haven." I left him standing in there and accepted the plate his mom made for me.

"ARIEL!" Haven shouted my name in anger. I turned and noticed him coming toward me. VJ handed Legend to Armonie and stood up.

"Why you yelling?" I rolled my eyes and put some mac and cheese in my mouth. I felt him yank my hair back and stick his tongue in.

"I knew your pussy was different." Everybody sucked their teeth.

"Thanks Ariel." He pecked my lips.

"She needs more food on her plate. Y'all know she eating for two now." Grams walked to me.

"You sure you're ready to have his kid?"

"GRAMS!" He shouted.

"What? I'm just saying Haven, we don't need another one of you." She shrugged and moved away.

"We're gonna go." Armonie said. I saw VJ placing Legend in his car seat.

"Why you leaving?" I asked.

"We've been here since this morning. I helped grams cook and I'm tired." I could see how tired she looked now that we're face to face.

"Ok. I'll stop by tomorrow." I walked over and kissed Legend on the cheek.

"Her nigga making her go." Haven said.

"My girl; you know your cousin, has a mind of her own. It's her choice to leave but this will be my last time here." VJ spoke with finality. Again, you could tell he was tryna calm himself down, but Haven wouldn't stop.

"Good. I can get back to seeing my family every week." Haven barked. All of us turned around. I saw VJ's facial expression and nodded to Brayden, who pulled up when we did. I wanted him to get close because VJ will flip.

"VJ lets just go please. I don't want y'all fighting." Armonie was tryna push him to the door. Colby Jr., Jax and the men stood up.

195

"You a bitch ass nigga." VJ said and put Legend down.

"THA FUCK YOU SAY!" Haven rose outta his seat.

"You heard me. Who the fuck finds out his girl expecting and instead of being happy, finds a reason to be a dick? Then your cousin leaving because she isn't feeling well and you assume, I'm making her.

"Fuck you nigga. You think because you saved her from the other motherfucker, I'm supposed to rock with you?"

"Nah because only a real man would appreciate what I did. The way I see it is, you're mad she didn't tell you and couldn't bring death to his doorstep. You want everyone to fear you but bro, you pump no fear here."

"VJ please." Brayden opened the door and Colby Jr and Haven's dad was holding him back.

"Armonie get out the way." Soon as her father said it, Haven swung, missed and caught Armonie on the side of her face. She hit the wall so hard, her body left an imprint and Legend almost fell out the car seat. If he weren't strapped in, he would've.

VJ looked down at them, somehow got outta Brayden's grip and hooked off on Haven. The two of them were going at it. Legend was screaming and Armonie's mom and I were tryna wake her up.

BOOM! Everyone stopped moving. Big Jax let the gun go off. VJ ran over to Armonie, lifted get up and carried her out to the car.

"Mrs. Banks please bring my son to the hospital." VJ asked and you could see a few tears leaving his eyes.

"What the fuck is wrong with you nigga? Huh? You knocked my sister out over your ass being petty. I swear if we weren't related, I'd shoot your ass between the eyes."

"Colby Jr." His father called out. He was just as mad and so was everyone else in the house. Haven fucked up this time and they were letting him know.

"FUCK THAT POPS." He went in the other room and grabbed his stuff.

"Armonie is his favorite cousin so I know it was an accident but so the hell what. He ain't have no reason to bother VJ. Now look. She back in the hospital and my nephew has to be checked out." He stormed out the house with his father, sister and brother. Mrs. Banks was in the car waiting.

"Let's go." Haven grabbed my arm and I snatched it away.

"What? You mad too?" Did he really just ask me that?

"Hell yea I'm mad. The shit ain't funny Haven." He wasn't laughing and I was referring to him bothering VJ. It's like he gets a kick outta messing with him and I think we're all over it.

"How would you feel if he treated me like that, punched me by accident and I dropped our baby?" He remained quiet.

"Exactly! You had no right to cause all this trouble." I picked my things up and asked his aunt Venus if I could ride with them to the hospital.

"We're over Haven. We can co-parent and I'll call you to go with me to the doctors but that's it."

"Well fuck you too Ariel." I stopped and turned around.

"What do you want me to do Haven? Huh? She's my best friend and has been before you. He's my cousin and I'm not gonna walk on eggshells or not be around him because of you."

"What the fuck ever. Bounce then bitch." Everyone in the house was at a loss for words like me. I walked up on him.

"I'm sorry you feel that way about me, but I won't let you stress me out. I wanted this baby regardless of what you believe. I hope by the time it's born you have a different attitude."

"Get rid of it."

WHAP! I smacked the fuck outta him. I've never in my life put my hands on a man. When he mentioned terminating my child, I snapped.

"How fucking dare you? You fucked this up, not me." I started punching him in the chest over and over.

"Let's go Ariel." His uncle Jax pulled me away and led me to the car. He told Venus to take me to check on Armonie and then home. As they spoke, Haven came out the house, hopped in his car and sped off. I don't even have the energy to

care if he crashes or not.

VJ

I paced the hospital floor a million times waiting on them to tell me if my son and girl were ok. When Monie hit the wall and passed out, all I saw was her ex abusing her again.

I jumped on her cousin and didn't give a fuck who got in it. I was over the childish shit he said and did. It's obvious he was testing me and even with my arm losing feeling every now and then, it didn't stop me from getting his ass.

The gun went off and I immediately ran over to her and my son. Legend was crying and he seemed to be ok but Monie was still knocked out, which broke my heart. She's been through so much and her own cousin accidentally hit her.

Even I know it wasn't on purpose, but he had no business swinging off anyway. Then, if my son weren't strapped in, he would've fallen out the seat and that had me hot.

I don't know who told them what happened but my parents, Ariel's and some of my cousins were pulling in at the same time we did. They all loved Armonie and stalked me for Legend to come over.

"Mr. Davis." The pediatrician came in to give me the results of the tests.

"Yes." She smiled and put her index finger in between my sons' hand.

"Legend here is going to be fine. He has a tiny scratch on his forehead which can possibly be from the tag on the seat or he may have done it. All the tests were normal and he's ok to go home." My mom stood and rubbed my back.

"Thanks. Is his mom ok?"

"Go check on her VJ. I'll stay with Legend and we'll be over when she gives me his discharge papers." My mom said.

"A'ight and pops don't hold him the whole time." He told me to leave. Him and Armonie were spoiling the shit outta my son. I thought it would be my mom, but my father can't seem to get enough. I mean he comes over everyday if we don't bring him by.

I told the doctor my mother could sign the paper work and thanked her for taking care of my son. I went into the regular emergency department and requested for them to buzz me in the back.

At first, they asked my name. I didn't know why until the receptionist said her mom has a name written down of a person who she didn't want to visit her. I had no doubt it was Haven.

"Where is she?" I asked her father who was sitting there with her siblings.

"My mom took her to the bathroom." Her sister told me.

"Is she ok? What are they saying?"

"She has a slight concussion and a busted lip." My fist balled up as her dad continued telling me what the doctor said. I leaned against the wall.

"Nobody blames you VJ. You had enough and did what you had to for your family." Her pops said.

"We good bro." Colby Jr said and gave me a man hug with his other brother. Her younger sister smiled and said I need to give Monie more kids because everybody being stingy with Legend.

"VJ?" Monie ran to me and I picked her up.

"You ok? You need anything?" She shook her head no and cried on my neck. Her family stepped out.

"Legend is with my parents. They're discharging him soon."

"Is be ok? Did he fall out the seat?" I closed the door and laid her in the bed.

"No. He has a scratch on his forehead. She said he may have done it himself; otherwise he's fine. Let me see." I moved the hair out her face and got mad all over again seeing her lip and the knot on her forehead.

"I'm ok babe. What about you?" She said her mom mentioned me and Haven fighting.

"Never worry about me. I'm good as long as you and my son good."

"I'm always gonna worry about my fiancé." She smiled and I couldn't help but do the same.

Last night after making love to her, I proposed. Yup, she had my son six weeks ago and I damn sure nut all in her so we could have another one.

She was lying on her side in front of me when I decided to pop the question.

"Monie, what you doing for the rest of your life?" She turned around and her mouth fell open. She lifted herself on her elbows and then sat all the way up. I opened the box and showed her the 10-carat princess cut, yellow diamond I purchased her two weeks ago. I got her the Tesla as a push gift, but I had yet to give her a gift of my own.

"It's been a long and crazy year, but I'd do it all over again if you're the woman it's with. In this short time, you had me fall in love with you, delivered my son and made me the happiest man alive. Would you do me the honors of being my wife?" She nodded and allowed the tears to fall.

"I won't mess up baby." I told her and put the ring on.

"I want to tell them at dinner tomorrow. Is that ok?" She asked staring at the ring.

"Anything you wanna do, I'm down." I kissed her and the two of us fell asleep holding each other.

She was supposed to mention it tonight but decided to wait when Ariel announced her pregnancy. She didn't wanna ruin the moment.

As of right now, my family are the only ones who knew and that's because my mom and aunt helped me pick the ring. I couldn't tell Ariel because she would've told.

"Do you still wanna marry me?" She looked up and wiped her tears.

"Monie that man don't dictate our relationship. Shit, if you wanted to get married right now, I'd go get the reverend guy who works here and do it. I love you Monie."

"I'm so sorry you're dealing with my cousin. I don't know what's wrong with him." I put both of my hands on her face.

"You can't worry about him; I'm not." She nodded and wrapped her arms around my neck.

"Here." I took the ring out my pocket and placed it back on her finger. She had it in the baby bag at her parents' house but again, she never got the chance to mention it.

"You got something to tell me?" Her father came through the door.

"I said yes." She smiled real big and flashed her ring.

"Oh my God. Sweetie you're getting married?" Her mom and sister ran over.

"You did good son in law." He and I had a discussion before I brought the ring. He voiced his concerns and I answered everyone truthfully. He gave me his blessing and now his daughter is about to be my wife.

"Treat her right." Colby Jr said and hugged her.

"Where's Legend?" Monie asked and we looked at the door. Ariel was walking him in.

"I'm sorry Armonie. I didn't know he was gonna act up." She started tearing up and handed my son to Colby Jr.

"What's wrong?"

"He told me to get rid of the baby because I said we were over." I felt Monie squeeze my hand and look at me. She mouthed the words *please don't leave*. Brayden had an aggravated look on his face as well. Haven is his best friend,

I'm his cousin and Ariel's his sister. I'm sure it's a lot for him to deal with.

"Ok Ms. Banks. I'm going to discharge you." The doctor scooted his way through everyone and gave her the aftercare instructions. They all stepped out while she got dressed.

"I'm gonna talk to him." I knew she meant her cousin.

"Not right now you're not." Her eyes met mine.

"He needs to cool off and accident or not, he needs to apologize to you Monie." She nodded.

"I'm serious. Not only did he hit you but he's making it uncomfortable for you when I'm there." I could care less but she didn't like the tension.

"You're right. Do you feel like taking a bath with me at home?" I knew it relaxed her.

"After I put Legend to bed, I'll do whatever you want." I smirked when she removed the gown and her breasts were bare. I loved sucking on her tities.

"Don't play Monie. You know I'll fuck you right here." She was massaging her own breasts and making soft moans. I lifted her on the table and was about to give her what she wanted. We heard the door open and stopped.

"You done?" Ariel asked.

"Yea. VJ helping me with my bra." After she put her shirt on, I opened the curtain and we stepped out. Once we got outside, it's like both of our families were there and we were having a party. The good thing is no one held a grudge toward the other over Haven.

"You ok honey?" Her aunt Passion ran over to her.

"I'm fine. Where's uncle Wolf?" She looked around.

"Him and your uncle Jax went to find Haven. When you left, he said some mean things to Ariel too." She looked at me.

"Don't even think about apologizing for him."

"I don't know why he's so angry."

"It's not for any of us to know but I don't blame you or anyone else and I don't want you blaming yourself."

"I'm trying not to but he's my son and..." She cried.

"Get your dramatic ass over here. The whole world knows Haven crazy so don't try and figure him out." Another woman said.

"Who's that?" I asked Monie. When I say it was a lot of people out here, it really was.

"My aunt Darlene. She's off the hook. Come on." I tried to carry her, but she said she's fine. Everyone ended up at my house drinking and having a good time. It made my fiancé smile and it's all I ever want for her. When they left, we put Legend to bed and took a bath like she requested.

****

"What the fuck you mean someone broke into the office?" I lifted Monie off my chest and sat up. We had Legend lying with us and I didn't wanna scare him.

"Mr. Davis, we're not sure how they got in but the office is destroyed and they took everything out the safe." Ashley said. She's the woman we left in charge down in VA. She came highly recommended and up until this very moment, we had no issues.

"How did they get in the safe? No one has the combination but me and my sister?" I picked my cell up and sent a message to Vanity.

"You're not going to believe this but per the security footage, they used some explosive device.

"You gotta be kidding me."

"I'm sending you the video now. The cops are still here as well. Is there anything you want me to tell them?"

"I'll be there shortly." I hung up and answered my cell for Vanity. After I told her what happened she volunteered to ride with me but I cut it short. I hung up with her and called my cousin.

"Yo!" The background was pretty loud.

"Where you at?" It was eight o clock on a Sunday morning, and he sounded as if he were at a club.

"Wifey wanted breakfast. You know these people talk loud as hell at restaurants. What's up?"

"I told him what happened as I got dressed. He asked if I wanted him to ride and I told him no. Mycah already text back saying he was waiting for me.

211

"I need you to check on Monie for me, if I'm not back tomorrow."

"You already know." I hung up, packed a few things and went downstairs where Monie was.

"I'm coming." She was packing a bag for Legend.

"Monie you need to stay home with our son." I appreciated how she had my back.

"What if the bitch sent someone there to do it and they're waiting for you. VJ you don't need to go alone." I stopped her from packing my son bag.

"I'll be back tomorrow or Tuesday."

"VJ something's not right. I mean all these years and you never had a break in. What if it's a set up?" I couldn't deny feeling the same way but until it's confirmed I couldn't say it's true.

"I'm gonna be fine. I'll even talk to you the whole way there." She was tapping her foot.

"Please let me go with you." She begged.

"Stop worrying Monie." I kissed her and fought with her about going, all the way to my car. She wasn't giving up.

"Go inside. I'm calling you." I showed her the phone dialing the house number.

"Please be careful." I kissed her and watched as she took her time walking to the door. We spoke the whole ride and once I got there, I had to hang up and call Mycah. He didn't answer so I sent him a text and went inside. The cops were gone but Ashley's car was still there. I walked in and Ashley had tears running down her face.

CLICK!

"Took you long enough to get here." My hands went up and when I turned around to see who it was, shocked wasn't the word.

Ariel

"What?" I opened the door for Haven. Neither of us called or sent a text message to the other all week.

"Move." He walked past me and sat on the couch.

"Is my cousin ok?" I folded my arms and stayed quiet.

"Ariel I'm not in the fucking mood. Is my cousin ok?" He barked.

"I shouldn't tell you shit but she's fine. You gave her a concussion and since she hit her face on the wall, her lip busted." He put his head back on the couch.

"You mean to tell me no one told you this entire time how she was?"

"My phones been off and I haven't been at work."

"What's going on with you Haven? Are you tryna make your family hate you?" He opened his eyes and looked at me.

"I don't care for him since that night in the restaurant."

"Haven it was your fault. Look." I plopped down on the seat across from him.

"VJ loves your cousin. I mean really loves her and she's not gonna invite you to her wedding if you don't stop this shit."

"Wedding?" He questioned.

"He asked her to marry him the night before the dinner and she accepted. Her intention was to tell everyone but you bullied me into taking a test and she didn't wanna spoil the moment." I went over to where he sat and lifted his face.

"She's never going to forgive you if you don't make it right with VJ." He didn't say anything.

"He's about to be her husband so if your plan was to scare him off because we all know per you and the guys in the family; no one is good enough for the women in your family but, he's not going anywhere." He chuckled.

"Mr. Banks gave his blessing. Haven its time you did too." I kissed his forehead and walked in the kitchen to get my food. I made a small meatloaf with mashed potatoes and string beans.

"Do I have to be his friend?" I jumped because he scared me.

"No. You never have to speak but talking shit and fighting him isn't the way to go. As you can see Monie will stay away and it's not fair to the family." I put some food on my plate and sat down to eat.

"Where's mine?" I blew on my food and ignored him.

"Ariel?"

"Haven, I didn't know you were coming and I'm still not speaking to you." I rolled my eyes.

"How you not speaking to me and we just had a whole conversation?" He went and got a fork out the drawer and started eating off my plate.

"You know what I'm talking about? How could you tell me to abort our baby?" I slammed the fork on the table and waited for him to answer.

"If you weren't gonna be with me, I wasn't about to let another nigga be around my kid." I shook my head because he's really crazy.

"Did you do it?" I ignored him.

"DID YOU?" He pounded on the table scaring me.

"No and stop doing that."

"Doing what?"

"Making me fear you. I don't like that." I never wanted to be in fear of a man I'm with. Monie went through it with Freddy and my aunt Maylan did with her ex too.

"My bad. Come here."

"No thanks." He gave me a look and instead of arguing, I stood in front of him. He lifted my shirt and rubbed my belly.

"How far are you?" He kissed it.

"Seven weeks."

"I felt the difference over a month ago so that's about right." I mushed him in the head and passed him the ultrasound photo.

"It looks like a pea." He was turning it upside down.

"You need to speak with Armonie." I started eating.

"I know. You coming?"

"Haven I'm not dressed and what you need me for?"

I sent a text to Armonie letting her know we were on our way because I'm not about to let him surprise her. She may not wanna see him right now and I hope VJ not there. If he is, she'll request to see him elsewhere.

217

She didn't respond so I finished eating. Afterwards, I went to see where Haven was, and he was passed out in the bed. I mean snoring and all. I sent a message back to Armonie and said, never mind we can do it another time because he fell asleep. I ended up getting in bed with him.

I don't forgive him just yet but I'm not gonna lie and say I don't miss laying under him.

****

RING! RING! I moved outta Haven's embrace to answer my phone. I don't know why I kept the old-fashioned ringtone. It's loud as hell.

"Hello."

"Hey Ariel. Carmen called out for the 7-7 shift for tomorrow. Do you mind covering?" My boss asked.

"Ok. I'll be there but I'm taking off for the next two days because it's my day off." I told her after looking at the clock.

"Ok. Thanks, and good night." I hung up, set the alarm for 5 am and went back to bed.

The next day, the alarm went off and it felt like I only slept an hour. I swear this baby had me tired all the time and these early morning shifts were killing me.

I got dressed, left Haven a note and headed to work. I text my boss this morning and she said I was working in the emergency room. It's where Carmen was scheduled. I couldn't wait for my dad's building to be done, and I could make my own hours.

I stopped at Dunkin Donuts on the way to grab a sandwich and coffee. I wasn't about to be there with nothing on my stomach.

"Good morning." I spoke to everyone and put my things away so the overnight staff can fill me in on the patients.

"Can we get a nurse outside. A woman brought her son in claiming he suffered a seizure." Everyone looked at me because I'm the only 7-7 staff here so far. It was 6:45 so they were about to leave anyway.

"I'm going." I walked out in search of the woman and noticed the security guy picking a kid up from someone's car.

I held the door and asked if he were the one who had a seizure? She said yes and I had security bring him straight back. Usually a doctor would come out but like I said, shifts are changing and he's not in an active seizure now, so I'll handle the triage part before the doctor comes.

"Hey lil man. Not feeling good huh?" His eyes were barely open, but he shook his head no.

"I'm gonna be right outside calling my friend." I nodded and took the little boy's shirt off and passed him a gown. I placed the thermometer in his ear and noticed his fever was 103.2, which is enough to cause a seizure.

"I need some Tylenol in here right away and can one of you bring me the cart so I can do bloodwork?" I shouted out the door and kept my eye on the kid.

"Ok. He's on his way." His mom said and walked back in the room.

"How long has he had a fever?"

"He wasn't feeling well last night. I checked on him this morning and he was shaking; his eyes were rolling, and he

220

had foam coming out his mouth." Another nurse came in with the cart and Tylenol.

"Did you call 911?" I asked.

"Did you see him pull up in an ambulance?" The woman got smart and me and the nurse Maria turned to look at her.

"Ma'am, I asked because some people contact 911 and leave. Then the ambulance is sitting at the house waiting for someone to open the door." I looked her up and down.

"And make that your last time getting smart with me. I'm trying to help your son." It took a lot outta me to remain calm. I understand she's probably scared for her son but no need her to snap on me.

"It's gonna hurt sweetie." After Maria gave him the Tylenol to bring the fever down, she held his arm while I took his blood.

"Good. My friend is here, and I don't think he'll be happy to know you got smart when you're supposed to be working." She walked out and I went to find her until Maria held me back.

"Who the fuck she think she is?" I whispered. Her son had fallen asleep and I didn't want him to hear me talking about his mom.

"Don't get yourself worked up. You know she must be miserable." We laughed.

"The hell you call me for, I ain't his daddy." I heard the voice and turned my head. I lifted the rail so the little boy wouldn't fall off.

"Stay here for a second." I told Maria. I didn't wanna walk out and the kid have a seizure and fall over.

"I'm not sure if I'll have a Co-pay or not and I don't get paid until Friday." This woman stood in front of Haven sobbing. Was he sleeping with her?

"Where the fuck is the money I gave you?" At this point everyone was staring.

"It was only two thousand and..." I cut her off.

"Haven you gave this woman two thousand dollars?" His eyes got big as hell.

"Yes he did and he gave me five before, not that it's your business. Why are you listening to our conversation?" All I could do is stare and he did the same.

"Haven why are you acting like we never slept together? It's been a year and..." The bitch was rubbing it in.

"You cheated on me?"

"Ariel." He reached out for me and I backed away.

"Cheated on her?" The girl covered her mouth like she said too much.

"Ariel?"

"Stop running Damien." I heard a lady shouting to her kid and didn't move fast enough. He ran straight to me and I fell face first on the ground.

Armonie

WAA! WAA! I rolled over to my son crying his head off. When I got off the phone with VJ, I ended up taking a nap with my son.

I looked down and his binky fell on the side of him. I placed it in his mouth, and he quieted down. I knew it wouldn't last long because he was wet and probably hungry.

After changing him, I picked my cell up and walked downstairs to get a bottle. As beautiful as the house is, I could do without all the steps. Granted, it's brand new and where VJ says we'd grow old in, but I may have to sleep downstairs when we older.

I fed my son, burped him, turned some baby show on and put him in the swing. I sat on the couch and picked my phone up to see if VJ called. When I noticed he didn't, it made my instincts kick in ASAP. He never goes an hour without calling and based on the time we hung up, it's been two. I didn't tell him I was taking a nap so it's not like he gave me time to sleep.

I called his phone and there was no answer. I dialed him again and again and still no one picked up. There's no way he wouldn't answer for me. My gut was telling me he's in trouble. I could go down there but I wouldn't know where the building was because he was in the hospital all that time. When he got out, he was home and then came here with me.

"Don't panic Monie. Don't work yourself up." I said to myself as I tried to think of what to do next.

"BRAYDEN!" I shouted to myself. I dialed him up quick.

"What up Monie?"

"When's the last time you spoke to VJ?" I asked already throwing some clothes on.

"Before he left for Virginia. Why?"

"Somethings wrong Brayden." I sat on the bed putting my sneakers on.

"WHAT?"

"I spoke to him the entire way to Virginia because he wouldn't let me go with him. He hung up to call Mycah and check on the office. I fell asleep and when I woke up, he still hadn't called. Brayden, I called his phone back to back and it's no answer"."

"Shit." He cursed.

"I told him to let me go. Somethings wrong Brayden." I started crying.

"A'ight. I'm about to go down there."

"I'm coming." I was downstairs putting Legend in the car seat.

"Monie he's not going to want you there if..."

"NO! I'm going. I'm dropping Legend off to his mom, so I'll meet you over there." He blew his breath and agreed.

I still had VJ's bag packed from earlier so all I had to do was stick some clothes in it. I locked the door and strapped Legend in the back seat. I used the Bluetooth to call my dad.

"What's up?" He answered cheerfully.

"I'm going to Virginia with Brayden."

"For what?"

"VJ went down there because someone broke in his office. He hasn't called me or answered my calls. I can feel it daddy. Somethings wrong." I felt myself going into a panic.

"Ok. Hold on. Relax Monie and tell me what happened." I explained and he agreed somethings off. They knew how VJ felt about me and he would've definitely answered the phone.

"I'm calling Colby Jr and Jax. They'll go with y'all."

"Brayden's..." He cut me off.

"They're going. Whatever's going on may require more help."

"Ok." He hung up and called me back a few minutes later to say they're on the way to his house to meet me.

I stopped at a red light and reached behind to put Legend's binky in his mouth. He always wanted it but spit it out a lot too.

"Where you at now Armonie?"

"At the light on..."

KNOCK! KNOCK! I rolled my window down and sucked my teeth.

"What the fuck you want?"

"Who is that?" I heard my father asking through the Bluetooth.

227

"How the fuck are you alive? I thought I killed you."

To Be Continued….